DEAD

LINE

A novel by JJ Gould

Published 2020
ISBN-13: 979-8561274015

Acknowledgements

Others may have a host of helpers to acknowledge. I have one. This book would not be written, edited or published without a lot patient advice from Rollan Wengert. Thank you!!

Chapter 1 - Charlie Hofer

It was the week after Christmas, and Charlie Hofer was in a foul mood. Charlie hadn't always been rich, but he'd always been loud, coarse, and profane. Over the years, he'd noticed that the richer he got, the more people were willing to overlook his flaws. But not that day. That was the reason for his mood.

Squat, florid, seventy-year-old Charlie had a lot of hair, but none of it was on the top of his head. He made up for that by letting the thin grizzled hair on the back of his head grow long and the hair on his chest bloom forth, a gray rat's nest with gold chains set off by unbuttoned silk shirts and expensive tailored suits.

"Get yer fat ass over here!" he said. The woman was certainly close enough to hear him, but he yelled it anyway, his voice surprisingly high.

"What's the matter, Charlie?" The woman tottered over, top-heavy and in high heels, ignoring his mood. Her first name had been Doris, but she changed it to Veronica when she started working for Charlie and then changed her last name to Hofer when she started living with him. Their common-law marriage had saved Charlie a ton on prenup.

"Read me this." He shoved an open envelope in her direction. Hofer had needed glasses for years but thought they detracted from his appearance, so as a nod to vanity and a way to exert control, he often made Veronica read him things.

The envelope was heavy linen, embossed, and she did not want to take it. "It's from them again?"

"It's from them again?" he said in a mincing voice, mocking her. "Who the fuck do you think it's from?"

Her voice took a soothing tone. "Charlie, you don't need these stuck-up jerks. You're too good for them."

He threw the envelope in her face. "What? You think you know what it says already? You think it's a no?"

The Oaks was not the only country club in Sioux Falls, but it certainly was the most prestigious. Sioux Falls was not a big city, certainly, but it did have a surprising number of millionaires. The most elite of these millionaires, who played golf and swam in comfortable seclusion, were known as the rich boys' club, and although they were not nearly as wealthy as Charlie Hofer, they snubbed him anyway. Four times, he'd filled out the application. Four times, he'd sweated his way through the meet and greet, trying not to seem as coarse as he was, trying not to be as profane as he was, openly hinting at how he would be willing to use his immense wealth to improve the club. They nodded smoothly and looked down at him smugly.

And now the letter had arrived again. He had an idea about its contents but wasn't completely certain. That made his foul mood even worse.

Charlie Hofer came from nothing. His dad had left a Hutterite Colony, and the family had been shunned. Young Charlie had used the fuel of spite to take advantage of a completely predictable human trait—sin. Starting with a run-down strip club on a state highway south of Aberdeen, Charlie targeted the hunters from out of state and the men coming in from out of town. He took the profits and added to them. He exploited other towns throughout the state that didn't have statutes expressly limiting his kind of clubs, and he built outside the city limits of towns that did. He sold sex, gambling, and booze in all the ways that were legal and in other ways that he could get away with. He built his brand by calling all the bars, stores, hotels, and strip clubs that he owned the same name: Goodies.

He bought billboards up and down the interstate that said, Have Some Goodies, then took those profits to diversify into video lottery, land, and motels. He'd married three times, always to strippers because he liked how they looked and the way they didn't understand prenuptial agreements. He was divorced and living with Veronica but was contemplating making it official. Being married might help his attempt to get into the club. The last time they'd met with the club, he referred to her as his fiancée. They had not seemed impressed.

Veronica held the expensive stationery, her lips moving as she read, her expression telling him the awful truth. *Rejected again.*

"Come on, Charie. Let's forget about it, huh?"

She tried to cozy up to him, but he shoved her away. "Those dog-shit sons of bitches… think they're better'n me. They're dirty as hell. They all are."

"Yeah, Charlie, I know." Veronica nodded wryly. Strippers knew all about men. "But what're you gonna do?"

Charlie sat brooding, a toad with a cigar and a Scotch. He brooded the whole day, staring at the TV, clicking through the channels, watching nothing. Then, in a flash of insight, he stopped and stared at the remote in his hand and burst out laughing, a sharp and venomous bark. And he began to plan. When the plan was complete, he started looking for the person to implement it.

Chapter 2 - Stan Martin

When the fateful letter arrived, Stan Martin was winding up another long day at News 610, KCHY, the Voice of Wyoming. There had been some snow in the morning, making for a treacherous drive to work, but by the time he pulled into the apartment parking lot, the sun had melted most of it. Jangling his keys, he opened the mailbox. He pulled out the letters and shuffled through them as he walked up a flight of stairs and down the hall to his apartment. If Stan Martin had taken the time to think about it, he would have realized he was a happy man. He had a job he was good at, a wife he loved, and a son to bounce on his knee when he came home.

Sadly, his job did not pay very well—he was the head of radio news at KCHY-AM in Cheyenne, Wyoming, the state capital and a pretty good place for a news director. As news director, he was in charge of three part-timers, known as rip-n-readers, who would rip the latest news off the wire-service printer, stack it in order of relevance, and read it twice an hour. That meant Stan not only had to read news in the morning shift, but he was also the sole reporter at the station—the only one required to actually find, research, write, and report news. As a reward for his diligence and professionalism, Stan was poorly paid, a reality he'd grown used to.

It was the end of the state legislative session, which consisted of about a month of relentless reporting of the various bills, budgets, committees, subcommittees, lobbying efforts, and press conferences—a long, long month but important to Stan's livelihood. Underpaid as he was, he furiously wrote story after story, sending them upstream to the wire service, and each story that was picked up would add a few more dollars to the check and a much-needed bit of moonlighting bonus money for his young family.

Family. The thought made him smile. Marriage and family had come late to Stan Martin's life, and he was grateful and proud of his new role as husband and father.

He checked the mail, grabbed the stack of what appeared at first glance to be mostly bills, and charged up the steps of the dingy building to the second floor, apartment 4B.

He turned the key in the lock and walked into the one-bedroom flat decorated in industrial shades of beige, tan, taupe, and oatmeal. Claire was holding the baby on her hip, standing by the stove. She looked up with a smile, and Stan's heart gave the same little jolt it always did. Claire would turn heads wearing a burlap sack.

"Ring baloney, boiled potatoes, and broccoli. You've got twenty minutes to enjoy it before I have to get to the diner."

"What did the doctor say?" Stan picked the baby out of Claire's arms and kissed his cheek. The baby stared back owlishly. The baby had a name, but they seldom said it—no need, really.

"He said sit down and eat your supper." She gave him a kiss and a nudge toward the kitchen table.

Stan nodded and sank into the padded vinyl chair, grateful to sit down and suddenly hungry. He bowed his head and thought a wordless grace. He was grateful for this woman who loved him and for a place to come home to at the end of a long day.

"Mail come?" Claire asked.

"Right here. Aren't you going to join us?"

A good daycare was hard to find and expensive, so Claire had gotten a job that fit around Stan's. The diner was open twenty-four hours a day, desperate for good help, and satisfied with Claire's arrangement of filling out her hours one week in advance.

The baby studied them both, first Claire, then Stan, who blew on a small piece of potato and held it out on a fork. The baby shifted his attention to the potato. Like a judge weighing a sentence, he pondered the fork before opening his mouth and allowing Stan to insert the food. Then he closed his mouth and chewed, looking from one parent to the other soundlessly.

"Weird," Claire said, voicing what both of them thought.

During all of his eight-month life, John Martin McGarvey had not uttered a sound. No crying, no burbling, no chortling, no cooing, no nothing. At first, they thought it was a blessing. Sleeping through the night was an almost immediate option for the two of them. Yet when Claire would wake up to check on him, he would be wide-awake. If she wondered if he might be hungry, he ate. If she was concerned that he might need changing, he did. If she felt like rocking him, he seemed to enjoy it. He would study her face and eyes with great solemnity and tenderness and never utter a sound.

"So," Stan said, stabbing a piece of baloney with a fork. "What did the doctor say?"

"He said he didn't know. He said we should get some tests. He said it could be autism." She said the word in a careful, offhand way, like it was no big deal, like she'd practiced over and over again until she could say it without a tremor.

"Autism?" Stan repeated the word to the baby, offering him a bit of broccoli, which the baby solemnly tasted and carefully spit out with a look of disappointment.

"I don't think that's it." Stan had done his own research, trying not to worry Claire while looking up various behavioral disorders at the community college library.

"He said it *could* be. He said there are about eight places in the country that could help us. That could help John." She was idly sorting through the mail, probably dreading to say out loud the names of all the expensive hospitals in all the expensive cities.

Stan looked at her. Claire would not look back. She bit her lip and brushed a wisp of hair behind her ear, a habit she had when she was thinking.

"Hey." Stan reached out and held her hand across the table. "You have to leave for your shift... you'd better spill it now."

"Johns Hopkins, some place in Cleveland, New York City, Boston... a lot of places too expensive for us."

"You said eight. Any of them closer?"

"Yeah, they said Hall-Hauptmann Hospital has a new clinic for kids like... for kids with behavioral stuff. I guess it's pretty cutting-edge stuff."

Stan sat back, thinking. Hall-Hauptmann Hospital was located out of Sioux Falls, South Dakota. For a time, he'd lived in South Dakota. In fact, he'd met Claire there. Moving there would be fine—maybe even necessary. Already, Stan was mentally preparing the steps he would need to take to find work and help his young son. He was trying to remember if he had any media contacts in that town when he heard Claire snort.

"What. Is. This?" She held up a piece of mail and looked at Stan accusingly.

"What?" Stan reached for it, and Claire pulled back her hand, eyes narrowed.

"You got a piece of mail—hand addressed—on strip-club stationery?"

Stan held up his hands innocently. "Don't look at me. Open it if you want."

"Oh, I will, buddy boy." Claire was not one to be trifled with. She ripped the end off the envelope and shook out the contents. Her narrowed eyes grew wide with surprise and disbelief.

"What is it?" Stan and the baby looked at her.

"It's from a guy named Charles Hofer. He's looking to start a news station." She scanned the letter with increasing surprise. She looked up, slack-jawed. "Stan, he wants you to apply!"

Chapter 3 - Harrison Hall

Dr. Harrison Benjamin Hall IV, reigning head of the Hall-Hauptmann Hospital, sighed theatrically. It would be so much easier to be just a doctor, one of the relatively nameless twenty-five hundred or so who wandered around the hospital and clinics, dispensing diagnoses, checking charts, eating in the hospital café, flirting with the nurses, and plotting their course to retirement.

That was not his lot in life, though. No, Dr. Harrison Benjamin Hall IV was doomed to a higher path and, as such, was master of all the dreary little decisions that trundled their way across his massive mahogany desk, an arcane overblown thousand-pound monstrosity that his grandfather had bought in the '30s. He'd tried to get it replaced by something more modern, a far more suitable Poul Henningson original that someone was auctioning off, but the budget people raised their eyebrows, and the auction came and went, and now he was stuck.

He was wondering who'd gotten the desk when the intercom on his desk chimed.

"I'm busy." His answer was patient and immediate.

"Yes, Doctor. Shall I try to reschedule Mr. Warner?"

Hall blew out his cheeks, feigning resignation. In truth, he'd been waiting for this meeting all day, even looking forward to it, but it wouldn't do if he showed it. He looked at his reflection in a nearby mirror and gave himself a martyred look. "No, no, let him in." He dabbed a bit at the loose skin underneath his chin, wondering if it was time for another procedure.

The door opened, and Chet Warner was let in. Warner was the fourth-generation owner of Warner Manufacturing. Not a majority owner, only twenty percent, but enough to allow him time to sit on the board of the Oaks Country Club and have a restored 1920s Tudor on the third hole. He would start each day with a brisk walk around the course, year-round, rain or snow, and end each day holding court by his stone fireplace in the winter and by his poolside in the summer.

Feeling secretly envious of Warner's trim physique, he walked over to stand next to him. Hall was taller. "Great to see you, Chet."

"And you as well, Harrison." Warner refused to call him *Doctor*, a slight that annoyed Hall but one he decided to overlook, considering the reason for the day's meeting.

"How did the selection process go?" Hall asked. Warner was chair of new admissions at the club, a job he took very seriously.

"Poorly."

Hall had expected that answer and couldn't wait to find out the details. He strolled to the bar and reached for a tumbler. "Drink?"

"A little early," Warner said, following closely to make clear that the protest was not to be taken seriously. Hall prided himself on his single malt Scotch, and Warner knew it.

"Ice?"

"Two, please."

Hall poured the Scotch, and the two men stood by the patio window, looking out and down the golf course. Snow had fallen. A white desert drifted between leafless trees.

"Planning a gathering tonight?" Hall motioned across the white fairway toward Warner's house.

"You know Sophie. Neither rain nor snow nor gloom of night. She's got a hot toddy recipe she wants to try out. Heavy hors d'oeuvres. Starts at six if you can make it."

The Oaks had been started in the late 1800s, when the original Halls donated eighty acres along the Big Sioux River for a "club of distinction." Once pasture and slough, the land had become the place where the wealthiest of Sioux Falls lived and played, with a complete golf course, tennis courts, community pool, and clubhouse and a twelve-foot wrought-iron fence all the way around it. The Hall House was no longer the biggest or grandest of the homes in the Oaks, but it did have the finest lawn and the best view. Hall kept one of his offices there and called this his home, even though technically the building belonged to the hospital.

Hall decided he couldn't wait any longer, though he tried to be casual about it. "So the selection had an issue?"

Warner seemed just as eager. "It was Hofer again."

Hall clicked his tongue. "Such a weasel."

"He brought that bimbo with him this time."

"The Goody Gal?" Hall turned to look at him, shocked.

Hofer was a sleaze king who made his money in sleaze and advertised sleaze up and down the interstates of South Dakota. He called all of his strip clubs Goodies and featured billboards with buxom women strategically lined up behind the two *O*s in the name. The most famous one eventually became Charlie Hofer's girlfriend, and apparently, she was the very one he'd chosen to bring to the selection meeting.

"Sophie about had a fit." Warner delighted in the horror of it. "Hofer said she was his fiancée."

Hall decided to ask. "What was she wearing?"

Warner shuddered and leered at the same time. "About half what she should've been... the rest of her was covered in about forty carats' worth of diamonds."

"You said no, of course."

Warner rolled his eyes. "I sent the letter last week, but my God, it's not like he shouldn't have known."

"Such a dirty little man. Why do people like him think that money can buy them stature?"

"Well, that's just it... I got the strangest little note in the mail the other day."

"From Hofer?"

Warner nodded. "It said, 'You'll see.'"

"That's it?"

Warner shrugged.

"Well, I certainly hope he doesn't waste his time with legal matters. He won't stand a chance."

"Agreed," Warner said.

"So what else could he possibly do?"

"Nothing."

The two turned to look down the golf course as the weak winter sun struggled to break through the clouds. Hall sighed comfortably. Finally, the Hofer problem was over for good.

Chapter 4 - Trent Wheeler

Trent Wheeler was the general manager of Hall Media. He liked it, mostly, but was often quoted saying managing a group of radio stations was like herding cats through a dog show—the cats hated to stick together, but it was their only chance for survival. Except that day, it looked like one of the sicker cats was going to get thrown to the dogs, and Trent could not be happier. He was heading down the main corridor of the second floor—which some long-ago wag had dubbed "the Hall hall"—to confer with the powers that be about the pending deal.

The Hall building was three floors tall and laid out according to progress. The main floor and basement held the offices and presses of the *Plains Beacon*, a daily paper that had survived the panics, floods, booms, and busts of Sioux Falls to become its sole newspaper. The second floor was originally the studio and staff of the mighty AM giant, 710 KHAL, the Voice of the Sioux Empire, ten thousand watts of news, weather, and sports—broadcast partner of the Spartans—and back in the day, host of Donny Dumont's polka band, featuring a dance floor and seating for two hundred. The station hosted Lawrence Welk on a regular basis and the traveling big bands when they came through town.

The third floor held the TV station KHAL and the better offices. The bigger media buys, client events, and photo ops were held there. All of it was part of Hall Media, a virtual monopoly of media coverage that had been grandfathered into protection by Senator Hall when he was chair of the Senate Committee on Commerce, Science, and Transportation.

Wheeler's turf was strictly second-floor stuff, managing the ebb and flow of radio stations. When Donny Dumont and his polka band disbanded and left, KHAL-FM showed up and took over the dance floor, and a big remodeling job was done. Then KHAB-FM—adult contemporary—and KHAC-AM were purchased and added, and the dance floor got halved again. Then KCHD was absorbed into Hall Media as a part of purchasing a juicy fifty-thousand-watt FM signal out of Harrisburg. An alphabet soup of radio stations now filled up the marquee in the lobby and was enough to hold down the market until the radio-station group across town—whose name was never mentioned—added two more stations to their team. In frustration, Hall Media bought up an AM-FM duo out of Beresford and shoved them into a closet and a production room with no remodel whatsoever. Finally, Hall Media had twice as many stations as anyone else in the market, and Trent Wheeler had to manage the chaos. Three did well in the ratings and in budgets, two others gamely fought to hold their positions, and the bottom three never lived up to expectations or budgets, which meant a quarterly ass chewing for Wheeler.

Until today. Trent whistled cheerfully as he contemplated the demise of his problem child,

KCHD-AM 1610. Eight hundred meager watts of static and problems were about to be told goodbye.

How times had changed. Back in the day, the world of radio ran on the AM dial, and FMs were tagged on as the bastard stepchildren in the early '70s. Now FM ran the world, and the strategy was to buy FMs to control the market and deal with the AM stations that were part of the purchase. AM stations struggled for relevance, staffs were slashed, syndicated programs were added, and equipment was left to struggle along.

Sales staffs were wise to the trends. It was easier to sell FM music stations, and the rates were better, which meant better commissions. AM stations were seldom sold anymore, which caused big headaches when budgets came around. When KCHD AM-FM was absorbed into Hall Media, the juicy fifty-thousand-watt FM started cranking out hot hits to the eighteen-to-twenty-five demographic, and the AM remained a syndicated music-of-yesteryear format, a seldom-sold format that sales reps preferred to give away, offering dozens of free ads every time a client purchased ads on the bigger stations.

Until today. Trent glided into the conference room two minutes early and helped himself to a bagel. *Better lay off the donuts.* He was pushing forty, and his gut wasn't responding to normal post-Christmas dieting like it used to.

Diane VanDenBosch, the company controller, came in shortly after. A lot of Dutch lived around Sioux Falls, and the stereotype that they were tightfisted was exemplified in Diane. VanDenBosch was her married name, but her maiden name was TenHaaken—Dutch to the hardened core.

"Who authorized bagels and donuts?" A smaller woman with sharp features, Diane spent words like they were dollars.

"I did." Wheeler wanted it to sound magnanimous, but it came out defensive. *Geez, lady, lighten up.*

"I see." She picked up a cinnamon bagel and sniffed it suspiciously then wrapped it in a paper napkin and put it in her purse. "Let me see the contract."

Wheeler slid it across the table. "Two hundred thou." He could have saved his breath. Diane would not have believed mere words, especially his. "Is Harrison coming?"

"*Dr. Hall* has business at the hospital." She spoke without looking up, focusing instead on the far more important contract in front of her.

"Anyone from legal?"

"They will have their chance."

Wheeler realized that this meeting for up to eight would be attended by just Diane and him. He reached for a donut and tried again. "Two hundred thou is a good price."

"Where's the transmitter?"

"South of town. Four-hundred-foot stick. Transmitter's a relic from World War II. Remember the radio school the Air Force had up by the airport? The transmitter is from that—war surplus. Still uses *tubes*, for God's sake."

Diane said nothing.

"New transmitter would cost at least forty grand." Nothing.

"The board is shot too."

He was about to explain what a new control board might cost when Diane poked at a line on the contract. "Who's Emilio Gonzales?"

Wheeler brightened. "He's the guy that wants the station. Wants to simulcast an evangelical Spanish station out of Texas." As shitty as the frequency was, Hall Media was loath to sell it to a competitor who might take any listeners or revenue away from their large share of the market.

Diane sat back. Her expression settled into peevishness. That was her most pleasant look.

Wheeler added, "He seems like a nice guy."

Diane was ignoring him and packing the contract into a briefcase, preparing for a more important meeting on the third floor. Her eyes focused on the donuts and bagels. "You ordered too many."

Wheeler rolled his eyes. "Geez, Diane! Look at the contract! I know for a fact that three years ago, we bought that whole combo for two hundred fifty, and now we can peel off an underperforming eight-hundred-watt AM for two hundred? This is a great deal!"

The COO stood, hefted her briefcase into one hand, and lifted the plate of donuts and bagels with the other. "I'll take these upstairs."

Chapter 5 - Emilio Gonzales

Emilio Gonzales was his real name, and he did speak Spanish, and he did sign the contract. However, he was not interested in a Spanish-speaking radio station or in evangelism, and he was especially not interested in freezing his ass off on the northern plains. What he was interested in was collecting fifteen grand in easy cash for fronting for the real purchasers of the frequency. Cutting close to FCC laws, the application was technically true—it would broadcast to the Sioux Falls community, it would focus on news, and it would target an underserved audience. And for one hundred twenty days, no one seemed to care or investigate the humble Señor Gonzales, which was just the way the real purchaser wanted it.

Chapter 6 - Stan Martin

Stan Martin sat uncomfortably in an uncomfortable suit and tie in an uncomfortable chair, having an uncomfortable interview with Charlie Hofer, the king of sleaze.

"Want some booze?" Charlie snapped his bejeweled fat fingers and reached for a crystal decanter.

"No, thank you," Stan said uncomfortably.

"Yeah, that's right, you're an alky." Hofer grinned. "No sauce for you—too bad." He motioned to a top-heavy woman in stilettos to pour for him alone. "You seen my fiancée, Veronica DuPont?"

"We've never met."

"Ho, but you've *seen* her—up and down the interstate. She's the Goody Gal." He pointed to her chest and leered. "See?"

Stan's face grew a bit hot. "Pleased to meet you, Miss DuPont."

The woman looked at him curiously but said nothing.

"Now, to business," said Hofer, sliding a contract across the table. "How's this look?"

So much for formalities. Stan looked at the number and raised an eyebrow. "It looks suspicious."

"How so?"

"That is easily four times the going rate for reporters in a town of this size, and it's only a two-year contract."

"I'm new to this business." Hofer failed to look innocent.

"But not new to business. You might as well tell me what this is about."

"It's about me starting a new business, a radio station." Hofer either raised his shoulders or made his neck disappear. "What's wrong with that?"

"And you want me to work for you… why?"

"Because you're the guy from Dansing, the guy who solved the murder of that rich heiress chick. And you're the guy that figured out who poisoned that other chick in Wisconsin. You're a reporter. You find out stuff."

Stan leveled his gaze at Hofer for a solid thirty seconds. Hofer squirmed a bit, pretending to be interested in his drink.

"You are Charlie Hofer. You are probably the richest resident of South Dakota. You have earned a fortune and a reputation. I found out that you are building the largest home in Sioux Falls, but you are not building it in the nicest neighborhood."

Hofer looked sullen but did not meet Stan's gaze.

"That neighborhood is the Oaks, a gated community where the very wealthiest live. I did a little asking around. The Oaks is a members-only club. You must be asked to join. I'm guessing you asked, and they said no."

"Those fucking mealy-mouthed bastards. Like their shit don't stink," Hofer snarled, his eyes small and glittering. Stan's guess had hit home.

"There is nothing illegal about gated communities," Stan countered.

"But there is some shit. There's always some shit." Hofer pounded the table with the flat of his hand, making Veronica jump. "Those bastards got a paper and a TV and a bunch a radio stations and a high-and-mighty attitude that nothing they do is ever gonna get found out." He leaned back, eyes triumphant. "But I got my own station now. And I got you, and I got the money to hire as many reporters as you can find to dig as deep and as hard as you want to find the shit."

Stan sat back. The cards were on the table. "So, say I do this. Say I set up an investigative news station. I will not break any laws or take any shortcuts. What if I search and ask and dig and, after months of effort, find nothing?"

It was Hofer's turn to sit back. "Don't worry, pal. You'll find it. There's prolly some shit goin' on at this very moment."

Chapter 7 - Dr. Harrison Benjamin Hall V

Dr. Harrison Benjamin Hall V paced outside the surgical suite, impatient and worried.

The surgery was scheduled for seven in the morning, and it was 6:58. *Dammit, dammit, dammit!*

LaCroix knew he liked to be on time, and he was purposely trying to toy with him and get him off his game. *Cocky asshole.* Hall was first in his class at Harvard Medical and a member of Mensa. He had a photographic memory. And here he was, waiting for a college dropout—a Southern hick with no background...

"Hey, Big Five... looks like I'm just in time."

Hall wheeled around, instantly relieved. Worry was replaced by anger. "No, you incompetent imbecile! You are late."

Devon LaCroix flashed just the right smile, a perfect mixture of contriteness and roguishness. "Big Five, you are right as usual. I have no excuse worth mentioning, just a little ice and snow and an accident on the Twelfth Street exit... you all prepped?"

The question was obvious, and so was the answer. Hall was swathed and masked and gloved, hands held up and away from the blue gown.

Devon glanced around and said quietly, "Need a boost?"

Hall didn't bother to answer. He jerked his chin, and Devon stepped in, pulled Hall's mask down, and expertly tossed the pill in, following it with a squirt of water. He replaced the mask and nodded toward the entrance to the suite.

"What do we have this morning?"

"Diabetic three F-er. Right hip." *Three F-er* was hospital slang for *female, fifties, flabby*. Now that Devon was there, Hall was starting to calm down, his nerves replaced by arrogance. "The surgical team is in place, and we have three scheduled for this suite."

Devon smiled again. "*Semper Fi.* Let's rock and roll." He lifted his own mask in place and backed through the suite doors, leading the way for the famous Dr. Hall.

Chapter 8 - Stan Martin

First things first. Charlie Hofer's experience in broadcasting was sparse and naive. There was usually a one-hundred-twenty-day wait between purchase and FCC approval. Normally, this waiting time was wasted, but Hofer had the money, the confidence, and the impatience to make use of it. He simply gave Martin a checkbook and carte blanche to make any decisions on getting a station up and going. April 1 was the deadline.

Stan started with the building. He decided not to tempt fate and look for a place downtown. *Too close to Hall Media.* Theoretically, a diverse introduction into a media market would sail through federal compliance, especially with a minority on the application, but Stan doubted the Emilio Gonzales story could withstand much scrutiny, and he fully respected the might and political power Hall Media could bring to play, so discretion seemed the best action for the moment.

Driving around town, he saw a For Lease sign in front of a three-story office building off of Cleveland Avenue. He pulled into the parking lot. *Three stories.*

It looked like the other tenants were a dentist, a real estate agent, and an insurance company. *Anonymous architecture, main entrance off the back parking lot.* He added it to the list.

There was a McDonald's down the street. Stan checked the time—almost noon. Claire had an appointment with a specialist at ten o'clock that morning, and they'd agreed to meet at the McDonald's for lunch.

Stan drove a 1970 Chrysler 300, matte black, that he called the Shark. It was hard on gas but had a powerful thrumming motor that was addictive no matter the mileage. He pulled out into traffic and then did a right into the McDonald's next to Claire's waiting truck.

They'd decided that two vehicles were absolutely necessary if he took the gig in Sioux Falls, and Claire immediately chose an extended-cab Ford pickup with a ladder rack, dingy white with some rust. She was adamant. "Not a beauty but solid mechanically, well below book, and it's what I will be needing."

Stan raised an eyebrow. "We're getting a truck?"

"Baby, a girl like me has needs, and I needs this truck." She'd flashed her dimples, and that was that.

Claire and the baby were in a booth. She waved him over and pointed at his waiting food. "Quarter Pounder with cheese. Water. No fries."

Stan smiled and nodded. He kissed her on the cheek and the baby on the top of the head, slid into the booth, closed his eyes, and was quiet for thirty seconds. Since meeting Claire, Stan never failed to thank God for the food he ate and the woman he loved and the family he had.

He looked over. Claire was halfway through her food, motioning to him with a fry. "Well, whatcha find?"

"You first." He nodded to John, anxious to hear what the specialist had said.

"I think our little man here has stumped the band. Not autism, not hearing loss." Claire ticked off the things it was not. "Plus a bunch of other nots I couldn't pronounce." While she talked, the baby stared at both of them. "When I said he never cries, the doctor said she wanted to do a little more research and set another appointment."

"Speaking of never crying, do you think he's hungry now?" Stan was studying the expression on the baby's face.

Claire cocked her head and looked at him. "Yes. Yes, I think he is." She picked him up out of his seat and reached for a bottle. "How about you? How's the search going?"

"Think I found a place. I'll swing by the realtor after this. That's the easy part. Now I'll have to find an engineer to wire the place up. Not easy since everyone I can think of does contract work for Hall Media."

"I have two cousins that do tower work… is that the kind of work you need done?"

"Some of it." Stan was eating his burger in small fastidious bites. "Have you mentioned them before?"

"Don't think so. Cal and Wes Cole. They travel around a lot. Solid guys. You'd like them, I think."

"Well, it's worth a call, anyway."

Claire held the bottle for the baby and continued eating fries with the other hand. "How much time before the license comes through?"

"Just over ninety days."

"Then what?"

Stan shrugged. "Then we start an all-news station with a focus on investigative news." He considered the baby drinking milk steadily from the bottle. "What was the name of the clinic?"

"Hall Clinic for Children. Part of Hall-Hauptman Hospital. Nice place. Big. Fancy. They must get a lot of endowments." Claire's eyes narrowed. "Why?"

Stan shook his head. "Nothing. Just that Hofer's got his mind set on some of these bigger businesses in town. Maybe Hall Clinic is one of them."

The baby looked at him.

Chapter 9 - Janet Brecht

Janet Brecht was suited and scrubbed up, looking exactly like the rest of the surgical team. She'd seen the assignment on Friday and knew she was working with Dr. Hall. Now she could see for herself what others had warned her about. As a surgical tech, she was low on the totem pole and knew it. She had taken a two-year course in the exciting world of medicine, which meant holding flaps of skin open while some high-paid jerk yelled at her because he could. *Oh well.* Ann Johnson was the other surgical tech. They knew each other from school and were work friends, sometimes hanging out after work to blow off steam and gossip.

Sean Clarke, the CRNA, number three in the pecking order, leaned over the patient to get her attention. "You ready, Midge?" he crooned. "How's that Elvis song go—'Love Me Tender'? Can you sing me a little?"

The patient smiled. Sean was a looker and a favorite among the patients. He must have found out she was an Elvis fan. "Love me…" murmured the patient.

"Aaannd… she's out."

Good thing too. The clock on the wall said 6:58 a.m., and if the gossip Janet had heard about Dr. Hall was right…

Bang!

The double doors to the OR blew open, and a tall and imposing figure stormed in. The girl at the nurse station—*Jennifer, Jessica?*—jumped. Janet was pretty sure this was her first week. Her desk was along the wall so she would be ready to call out for help or support if the doctor needed anything. She didn't have much to do, but her schooling put her above Janet and the other scrub tech in the pecking order, even though she looked like she could still be in high school.

"Is she out?" Hall shouted at Sean Johnson.

"Yes, just now."

"And so is the doctor," said Ann Johnson. No sooner had Dr. Hall barked his question than he stormed out of the operating suite.

"What the…?" Sean asked. Eight sets of eyes— the only part that could be seen beneath scrubs, masks, and goggles—looked at each other.

"Shoulda known." Ann's voice was dry. "When I saw Devon LaCroix's stuff here but no Devon, I knew he'd freak."

"Who's Devon LaCroix?" Janet hadn't heard the name or seen it on the staff list.

"He's a sales rep for Panco. Mainly hips and knees," Sean said.

"Ohh, Devon is way more than hips and knees." Ann's eyes twinkled.

"He's a cutie?"

"Oh, honey. He's ex-military. Was a medic. He's got that charm and swagger and…"

The swinging door burst open again, and two blue-clad figures entered the suite—the taller Dr. Hall and an energetic figure with… yes, a definite swagger.

"All right, Big Five. It's showtime!"

That was not the thing for a rep to say before a surgery, but it did not faze the doctor. In fact, it seemed to comfort him. Dr. Hall was a nervous sort. His eyes darted around at each of the utensils on the tray, a tic in one eyelid. "Are we ready?"

The way he said it made Janet uneasy, like he wasn't sure if *he* was ready.

Sean gave the vitals.

"Sc-Scalpel," Dr. Hall said.

Janet handed him the scalpel then shot a glance at him. The guy looked like a nervous wreck.

Tentatively, he made his first incision. "Right here?" The way he said it made it sound like a question.

The PA, a heavyset guy named Morrison, seemed alarmed. Technically, he was number two, the one who could handle any procedure and step in if needed. That day, he looked a little ill.

The next six hours were horrific. With each incision, the doctor became more and more tentative, often pausing to stare at seemingly nothing. Sean, the anesthetist, looked worried. The longer patients stayed under anesthesia, the more problems arose in post recovery. Janet had seen this hip replacement done in as little as fifty-five minutes by other surgeons. The suite was booked for three procedures that day. One for sure would have to be cancelled.

Morrison, the PA, looked pale. He was sweating. After three hours in, unbelievably, the original hip bone had yet to be removed. Suddenly, Morrison collapsed.

"Hey there, big fella!" Devon was the first to react, stepping in from behind. He grabbed Morrison around the waist before he fell completely and pulled him off to a bench along the wall. Technically, the sales rep was to be confined and away from the patient, behind his table of sets which included every imaginable joint, plate, screw, and accessory, all sanitized and ready to go.

"Musta been somethin' I ate." Morrison looked glassy-eyed and out of it.

Janet felt a little panicky herself, like she was watching a car wreck in slow motion. She looked at the patient with a pang of remorse. *Sorry, lady.* Then she looked at Dr. Hall. *Oh shit.*

The doctor was losing it, and everyone in the OR could see it. He wasn't focused on Morrison or the patient—his eyes were locked on a point in the middle distance, staring at nothing.

It was Devon who reacted first. He started in with his patter, slow and soothing, the tone more important than the words. "Hey, Big Five, piece of cake. You just gotta grab that saw and whack the bone through right about there." He pointed with a laser pointer. "Just like eighth-grade shop class. Easy peasy."

Woodenly, Dr. Hall followed instructions, LaCroix talking him through what he must have seen done thousands of times.

"She looks like an eight centimeter, Doc. Perfect! Got the right size right there, third drawer down." Again LaCroix pointed with the laser pointer.

It reminded Janet of those airliner movies where the air traffic controller talked the panicked passenger into landing the jumbo jet. Four and a half hours into the operation, Dr. Hall was still fumbling with the artificial hip joint, awkwardly trying to seat the joint in place with a four-thousand-dollar stainless-steel hammer. He swung and hit it off center with a cracking sound. Janet could see where the femur had split off a six-inch wedge of bone, now white and bloody.

"Shit!" Hall said.

The doctor was really freaking out, and again, Devon stepped into the void with a patter of words. "Happens all the time, my man. Three times last week alone. That's what I've got plates and screws for. Slather some bone cement on it, and she's bulletproof, better than before. Fourth tray down. Get 'er done with three number-four plates and about twenty-four screws, depends on how tough the bone is… the bone cement is right there… like a walk in the park with a beauty queen."

"You do it." The tone of the surgeon was like that of a spoiled boy who wanted to go home.

The surgery team stopped and stared. Morrison looked up weakly from a nearby bench.

Dr. Hall stared defiantly at LaCroix. "You heard me, you cocky son of a bitch. You know everything. You point from back there like you are God's gift. You do it."

His hands were shaking badly. Everyone could see it. Devon looked at Sean the anesthetist. Sean in turn looked at the monitor over the patient's head. The vital signs had been artificially slowed down far too long for a simple surgery like this.

LaCroix exhaled long and deep. "All right, Big Five. Been a rough morning all around, so let's just do this." He stepped out of the room.

The rest of the team stood frozen in place, all eyes staring at Hall, whose hands were shaking so badly he had to fold his arms. The nurse at the station by the door had her hand poised by the phone but seemed paralyzed. The only one who seemed relaxed was LaCroix, who had come back in, scrubbed and ready.

"Hey, Big Five, why don't you help out your number two, huh?"

Stiffly, awkwardly, Hall stepped over and perched next to Morrison, seemingly oblivious to the room around him.

"Well, how's this for a clambake, huh?" Devon stepped up to the incision, completely confident and in charge.

Calmly and smoothly, making a little patter and gentle banter with the team, his hands steady, his movements quick and certain, LaCroix landed the plane, just like in the movies. No muss, no fuss, not a bump or squeal of the tires. He expertly set the plates, squeezed in the cement, attached the screws, and tapped the joint home.

"Nothing but the needle and thread now, girls, like sewing a 4-H apron," Devon said, and Janet could see the experience of a medic at work, fast and nimble, clean and quick. Dr. Hall stood stock-still, catatonic, as the sales rep finished up the surgery. Devon nodded to Sean. "Bring her up, buddy."

And then with a final shuddering sigh, Dr. Hall walked out of the OR, followed by LaCroix, who was helping along the pale PA. The surgery team avoided eye contact with each other. Janet immediately reported herself sick for the rest of the day and went to find a bar near the mall.

They hadn't planned it, but there was Ann Johnson, too, sitting at a booth in the back, face white with shock. "You sick too?"

Janet said nothing until she'd gulped the entire contents of a Long Island iced tea and ordered another one. "Holy shit."

Chapter 10 - Claire

"Whaddaya think, kiddo?" Claire hoisted the baby up on a hip and continued her inspection of the house.

When they decided to move to Sioux Falls, both Stan and Claire had been skeptical of a long-term proposition. "Money like that, though?" Claire said. "You'd be crazy not to take it."

Stan agreed. "What about you? With this salary, we won't both need to work. What do you want to do?"

"I've got an idea," she'd said.

And that idea was the purpose of this house visit. The realtor hovered near the entrance, with no interest in actually going inside. "It's got good bones!" he called. "A real fixer-upper!"

Claire was doing some math in her head and ignoring his vapid comments. Sioux Falls was a growing city, usually in the top ten for economic growth nationwide. The house was on South Phillips, and its former owner had let it slip into decay. The front yard was a forest of overgrown trees and shrubs, the antithesis of a place with curb appeal.

Half a block to the north, there was a definite uptick in the look and maintenance of the homes.

And despite the realtor's hackneyed comment, the house did have good bones. It was a two-and-a-half-story Craftsman, probably mid-1920s with what looked a major upgrade in the '50s where the attic had been converted to a large dormered room with leaded glass and wood floors. The house had clearly been a beauty back in the day. If the town continued growing, the nicer neighborhood would easily migrate south and encompass this block too.

"Why are they selling?" Claire asked over her shoulder.

"Estate sale." The realtor, his arms folded across his chest, gingerly stepped into the doorway. He looked warily at the dingy interior. "The three kids live on both coasts and have no plans on coming back. They want it to have a good owner. A young family like yours."

Claire rolled her eyes. *Time to start digging.* "Well, let's do a little looking around and see what we can find."

Ninety minutes later, the realtor looked haggard and defeated.

"Termite tracks, horizontal foundation crack, bat droppings in the attic…" Claire ticked down the list. "An eighty-amp service, forty-year-old furnace. Looks like the air conditioner is an old swamp cooler. That thing should be in a museum somewhere."

"It has such potential, though." He sounded like he didn't believe his own words.

Claire's narrowed eyes glinted steel. "Well, that potential is going to have to come out of their end, not mine." She shot him an offer.

He didn't blanch. He must have been showing the house for a while. "I'll talk to the family and let you know."

Chapter 11 - Sean Clark

The nurse anesthetist, Sean Clark, was coming out of OR when he got the page. "Sean Clark to Central Four, Sean Clark to Central 4." He got about four pages a day, usually routine stuff or a phone call, but Central 4 was for post-op conferences with families. He felt a tremor in his gut. *Uh-oh.*

Normally, the surgeon or the PA handled the post-op stuff. When an anesthetist was called down to meet a family, it was either because the surgeon was busy in another surgery—rare—or because they and everybody of higher rank were avoiding the family and kicking the shit downhill.

Oh-uh.

The older of the two men looked confused, frightened, and out of place. He had a striped work shirt that said Earl on the patch and calloused hands with the grime worn in. "You know anything about my Midge?" He looked about to cry. "She had surgery this morning but hasn't seemed like herself. It's like she don't know me." He whispered the last part as if afraid of saying it out loud.

The younger man was equally upset. "It's okay, Uncle Earl. This can happen. Sometimes people react differently to anesthesia... Aunt Midge is just a little slower than some at recovery." Turning to Sean, he became more professional. "Her name is Martha Elaine Sanderson. Midge is what everyone calls her. Fifty-eight. Left hip replacement. The surgery was this morning. I just got here myself. Were there any complications?"

Oh shit.

"Yes, there was a fragmentation of the femur, and some extra plates were required. Not ideal, but she should be okay."

"Can we talk to the surgeon?" The younger man checked a pad of paper. "Let me see... Dr. Hall?"

"Dr. Hall is away with other patients. I'm not sure when he will be able to visit with you."

The younger man was trying to soothe his uncle and threw out an icebreaker. "Hall? He any relation to the Hall Clinic Halls?"

Sean nodded nervously. "Yes. Fifth generation."

"Oh! See, Uncle Earl? I'm sure Aunt Midge was in the best of hands." He smiled encouragingly to both Sean and the older man.

Earl sniffed hopefully. "Y-You think so, Bill?"

The younger man was freckled, open faced, sandy haired, and athletic. He looked like he could be a tennis instructor or gym teacher. He nodded again. "You bet, Unc! And I'm sure when I come back down day after tomorrow, she'll be right as rain." He turned to shake Sean's hand. "I've got to head back up to the Cities tonight, but I'll come down Wednesday to see the doc then. In the meantime, I'll have my receptionist send down for the charts. Oh, here." The tennis pro fished into his pocket for a card. "Maybe I can talk you into the nickel tour when I come back. I always was curious how you run things down here."

The card said: *William C. Sanderson, MD, Doctor of Orthopedic Surgery ABOS/AAOS/AANA.*

Sean's heart skipped a beat. *Oh shit.*

Chapter 12 - Stan

Stan Martin had the papers signed on the radio station building, a ten-year lease on a fifteen-hundred-square-foot office underneath a dentist and behind an insurance agent. Since it was hidden in a mostly residential area sharing a parking lot with an apartment building, Stan doubted anyone would expect a radio station. The lease paperwork had been signed by Emilio Gonzales, whose English was normally excellent but if needed could become clouded and heavily accented. When asked about his business, Gonzales enthusiastically praised God in a torrent of Spanish, pumping the real estate agent's hand enthusiastically.

She nodded awkwardly. "I see."

The agent scanned the paperwork as if looking for clues. The location had the proper zoning. The station would have between five and ten employees and between one and five customers daily. Her face cleared as she spotted the cashier's check in the full amount clipped to the contract. One year paid in advance.

She smiled brightly, carefully said, "Buenos dias," and left with the check.

Welcome to America.

Once gone, Stan shook Emilio's hand. "Thanks."

"You got it, pal." Gonzales's accent was now completely gone. "We done now?"

Stan nodded. "Yep."

"Adios." Sounding more Texan than Mexican, Gonzales turned and left, his job done.

Now for the remodel.

Chapter 13 - Janet Brecht

Later on, Janet and the other members of the surgical team would call it the "Get-our-story-straight meeting," although that was certainly not what the two attorneys and the two doctors Hall called it. The meeting had taken place in the office of Dr. Harrison Benjamin Hall IV, a large expanse of wood, leather, cut glass, and collector's volumes behind more beveled glass. In the middle, next to a fireplace, sat the members of the surgical team on deep, plush, dangerous carpet, looking up and across the table at the doctors Hall and two lawyers, Everett Meyer—a jovial attorney with a smooth rich voice and the eyes of a shark—and an attractive woman in a charcoal business suit with the same shark eyes.

Cozy.

"Well, well, we might as well start." Meyer, who was running the meeting, chuckled mirthlessly after five minutes of strained introductions.

"This—this *practice* of law, this *practice* of medicine that we are called to…" Meyer paused, searching for the right words as if setting his trap carefully. "It seems so simple when we are young, so clear-cut. Every situation seems to have been studied and explained either in a book of law or"—he gestured to the books behind glass—"in a book of medicine." He steepled his fingers and puffed out a ponderous sigh. "Yet it is not simple or straightforward, nor is it black and white."

The woman next to him was scribbling furiously on a legal pad, the scratching of her pencil the loudest sound in the room.

"Without muddying the waters with either medical or legal jargon, let us revisit the tragic circumstances that surround the unfortunate Martha Elaine Sanderson." Meyer looked over his glasses at the papers in front of him. "It seems that the operation to replace Mrs. Sanderson's left hip was going smoothly until the femur split, causing the need for more plates and screws to be added. This rare occurrence caused some need for additional time under anesthesia while the correct medical hardware was selected and attached, and then the hip replacement was continued. Dr. Hall the Fifth"— Meyer gestured to a pale and glassy-eyed Hall— "commends your excellent teamwork in pulling together in this difficult surgery. Certainly, the family is upset, and although anesthesia is itself a practice— one that with continued *practice* has become most reliable—it, too, is not foolproof. And, Nurse Clark, as the person in charge of the anesthesia and the one ultimately responsible, I want to assure you that the full legal team of Hall Clinics stands by to protect you in any legal or other inquiries. I can't imagine what the burden would be financially and professionally on a nurse who would have to face scrutiny alone without expert legal consultation."

Janet glanced over at Sean, whose face was frozen and unreadable. The threat was obvious, the scapegoat named.

Meyer said smoothly, "So before we agree and sign the testimony I've read to you all, do any of you who were present have questions?"

There was a long, leaden pause. Then dry mouthed, Ann Johnson asked, "W-What about the sales rep?"

Meyer fixed a stare at Ann. "Sales rep?"

Ann Johnson cleared her dry throat. "Yes. He, uh, he was there. Does he sign this?"

No one spoke. The woman stopped writing on the legal pad and murmured something in Meyer's ear.

"Oh." Meyer leafed through the papers. "There was a medical-equipment representative for Panco, Devon LaCroix. He was the one who provided the trays of equipment to Dr. Hall before surgery. Of course, he was not in surgery—records show he checked out of the building at"—Meyer checked—"6:50 a.m. Ten minutes before Mrs. Sanderson's operation. He was not there at all." He paused and looked at each of them slowly, one at a time. The weight of silence grew heavy. "Are there any other questions before we sign?"

There were none.

"Good." Meyers's smile was wide and empty of any humor. "After a traumatic event like this, I suggest we all take the day to think about the frail and uncertain lives we all live. God bless you."

Later, Janet found herself at the same mall bar she'd gone to after the original surgery, drinking her third Long Island iced tea. *Holy shit.*

Chapter 14 - Stan

Stan Martin was the type to enjoy the English language and liked to keep arcane words from slipping off the table. For this reason, he took double pleasure in dandling young John on his knee. The little guy made no sound and still looked as serious as a judge, but Stan sensed he liked it as much as Stan did.

"Cute little feller."

The kid who made that comment had an accent as thick as a Louis L'Amour character and, in fact, resembled one as well—mid-twenties, lean through the hips, wearing cowboy boots and western shirt. Probably no more than one hundred sixty pounds but sinewy, like he could work all day. It was obvious that the kid next to him was his brother. They weren't twins but were so close in appearance and age that Stan could not tell which was the older.

The other kid smiled and nodded. "Yep."

Claire was sitting at the kitchen table in the apartment they were renting, and she looked like she could be a sister to them. Same wiry build, same relaxed, calm, no-nonsense look. She continued the conversation over a piece of scratch paper. "See, the house is solid, built in 1924, but the basement is shot. Cracks in the foundation and some termite tracks." She had the lot sketched out on the paper. "But as you can see, it's a double lot. I figure we can dig a new foundation next to it and move the house onto it. There's a drop-off to this side big enough for a walkout, maybe a second entrance."

Stan raised an eyebrow. "That seems pretty ambitious."

"But doable." Claire looked confident.

Her cousins seemed in agreement. "Yep."

Claire pointed to one of them. "Wes, here, was a slip hippy for a summer, helping pour concrete for silos. Slip forms, you know? The kind where you start with a ring at the bottom and just keep slipping the form up higher and higher till it's done."

Wes seemed content to let her do the talking.

"And Cal did some general construction for a couple years too. Knows his way around."

Cal said, "I do, some."

Stan started to object. "I thought you brought these guys here to talk about the radio station."

Wes nodded again. "That too." He reached for the baby. "Do you mind? I always liked babies."

Stan handed him over, and Wes chucked John on the chin and made a clicking sound like he was riding a horse. The baby studied him seriously while Wes continued. "Cal and I worked with some tower jockeys for a year or so—helped set up a station by Butte, run up the tower, a thousand-foot FM job, and then wired the place for electricity and studios too."

Stan was surprised. And a little skeptical.

Wes read the look. "We know what we're about, mister."

Stan raised a hand. "No, no. I get it. You just seem a little young to know all this stuff."

Cal grinned calmly. "We're fast learners."

Wes was making a face at the baby. "Yep."

Claire chimed in. "And they can check in and maybe give me a bit of help or advice at the end of the day. I said they could have the other bedroom and kick in a little rent."

It was obvious Claire had been doing a lot of thinking, and Stan knew enough to let her do it. He shrugged and offered, "It's still a big job. You're going to need some other help."

Claire smiled. "Oh, sweetie, I've got that all figured out."

Chapter 15 - Jessica Wright

There were thirty-three attorneys who looked after the well-being of Hall-Hauptmann Hospital, the clinic, the media, and sundry other ventures, and Jessica Wright was the lowest on the totem pole.

"Rosie!" her granddad had said. He was the only one who called her that. "Forget teaching! You've got the brains for it. Why not law school?"

So off she'd gone to the University of South Dakota, where a law degree was still affordable and where South Dakota businesses trolled the graduating classes for the best and brightest. Seven months into her career, she was learning a whole lot more than her professors had ever taught her. Especially that day.

She was fast with a pencil—she'd taken shorthand as a summer school course at the high school in Pierre, since her dad said it might come in handy—so she'd been tagged to back up Everett Meyer's tape-recorded meeting between the doctors Hall and a bunch of very nervous nurses. Once the meeting was over, she'd shoved the stack of papers and the legal pad into her leather briefcase—a law school graduation gift. She was hurrying alongside Meyer down the hall to the hospital parking lot.

"They seemed kind of nervous." Jessica was fishing a little bit. She might have been green as grass, but there was definitely something wonky about what she'd just witnessed.

"Yes, they did." Meyer seemed pleased. He looked at her out of the corner of his eye as if trying to decide. Jessica had seen that look before on older men who thought money made them attractive.

She gave him a look back. *Don't even think about it, buddy.*

He was smart, anyway—she had to give him that. Meyer instantly made his expression more professorial. "It's important that all the people we represent know the importance of the law and that justice is nothing to trifle with."

He moved his leather attaché case from one hand to the other to check the time on his Rolex. Maybe he wanted to know what time it was, or maybe he wanted Jessica to see the dazzling watch that was worth more than her annual salary. Then he paused at the doorway to the parking garage. March in South Dakota could still be quite nasty, and Meyer had no coat.

Jessica decided to level with him. "It seemed like some of them were maybe lying or at least hiding the truth. What does the law say about that?"

"The law is gray on that."

"And what if we think they are lying?"

"It's gray on that too."

"What if we find out for sure they are lying?"

Meyer smiled pityingly. "My dear, the beauty of the law is that it is all the same color: gray."

Jessica grew stubborn—a little streak from her rancher granddad. "If any of them are lying, and it gets out, then what are we supposed to say? What are we supposed to do?"

Meyer opened the door. The meeting was almost over. "If—let's say *if*—what you presume is true, no one in that room would be stupid enough to talk about it."

Chapter 16 - Deidre Hall

Deidre Hall might have married into the Hall dynasty, but there was no doubt who ran the show. She looked with contempt at her husband and stepson. "You did *what*?"

Harrison avoided her gaze and plucked at some nonexistent lint on his cashmere sweater. "I told you, Meyer took care of it."

Deidre stepped close to him, forcing him to meet her eyes. "No, you did not tell me about Meyer. You did not tell me about the meeting. You did not tell me about this"—he pointed to the younger Hall—"failure."

The younger Hall tried to bristle at the word but could only cringe out a defense. "It could've happened to anyone! She was obese and had poor bone health…"

"Shut. Up." Her sharpened fingernail kept pointing at the younger doctor, but her eyes remained locked on her main prey. "I've warned you about this, Harrison. You are to tell me about such things before you tell anyone else." She raised herself to her full height and looked him in the eye. "You must be punished."

His eyes widened in a mixture of fright, shame, and excitement. "Yes, Deidre."

Chapter 17 - Benjamin Hall

When Dr. Harrison Benjamin Hall V was a little boy, he had no idea about his family legacy. He was just Benjy, a lonely kid in a big house, with a stable of matronly and slightly disapproving nannies. The first thing they took from him was his name. When he got older, he was told that *Benjy* was too juvenile and suggested that Ben was a possibility and Harry was never a possibility.

He also learned that his career options were severely limited. He was a Hall, not just wealthy and honored but also obliged to carry on the name started by Harrison Benjamin Hall in the post–Civil War years. The original Hall had been an eager and ambitious young man who moved to Sioux Falls— Dakota territory—to ply his trade in the booming businesses of divorce and alcoholism.

Because of lax territorial laws, wealthy and unhappy husbands could take up residence at a luxurious hotel in the burgeoning town of Sioux Falls and file for residency and divorce. Ninety days later, they could leave as free men… free from wives perhaps, but not from alcohol. The recent horrors of the Civil War left many veterans medicating themselves with large quantities of alcohol, an affliction so common that it was known as "the soldier's disease."

Young Harrison Benjamin Hall was an intern for the famous Dr. Leslie Enraught Keeley, inventor of the "gold cure" for alcoholism. Hall was impressed by the men's desperation to be free of the disease and the amount they were willing to pay, so upon moving to Sioux Falls, the first thing he did was hang out a shingle for what he called "the ivory cure." Soon, he had a big enough trade to build his own clinic and hotel on Phillips Avenue, with alcoholics on the dry, austere second floor and divorce seekers on the opulent, wet first floor.

The young and prosperous Hall soon branched out into other endeavors, including politics and the press, picking up an influential family through marriage and lucrative land investments through chicanery and connections. By the time Harrison Benjamin Hall Jr. arrived, the original Hall was the editor of the largest newspaper in the territory and one of the first senators of the brand-new state of South Dakota. And the Hall empire continued on its inevitable way, content to be a very large fish in the small pond of South Dakota.

Decades and generations and history kept piling up until more than one hundred twenty years later, the family empire landed squarely on top of young Benjy with its pressure, expectations, and criticisms. His father especially. Hall the IV, as Benjy called him, gloried in the name and power of those on the inside, intoning the need for the fifth generation to carry on the obligations of his family, pompous and domineering.

Until Deidre. Hired as a nurse at Hall-Hauptmann, her goals were much higher. She was a stunning beauty, tall and statuesque with ice-queen-platinum hair and witch-green eyes. Within one week of meeting the Fourth, she had him wrapped around her long fingers. Cooing and beguiling one day, aloof and snappish the next, Deidre had him on his knees in short order.

He was besotted and, within five months, had dropped his wife of fifteen years and proposed marriage with a ring of colossal carat weight. She took the ring with one hand and grabbed his face with her sharpened fingernails in the other. Benjy watched in fascination as she locked his father in a long kiss, nails digging into his flesh, blood dripping down his cheek and chin.

About a year later, after she'd moved in and had the whole house redecorated, he heard them one night yelling and screaming. Curious, he crept down the hallway and saw them through the open bedroom door. His father was trussed to the bed, naked, while Deidre, also naked, whipped him with a leather strap.

Benjy stared, astonished and aroused. Deidre looked up and saw him through the crack in the door, her face triumphant, like she'd been expecting him. Benjy stole back to his room, still ashamed, still aroused.

Later that night, his door opened, and Deidre, wearing nothing but a diaphanous robe, floated in to stare down at him. The robe slipped off, and she threw back the covers, exposing cringing, excited Benjy.

"Now it's your turn," she hissed and cut a line down his belly with her fingernail.

Chapter 18 - Claire

Claire pulled up her truck next to WorkReady, the day-labor place that looked like a Laundromat on the outside and smelled like disinfectant, stale cigarette smoke, and despair on the inside.

It was nine o'clock in the morning. About twenty people were lounging about the place, waiting for work. About half of them looked like they were hoping work wouldn't show up.

Sioux Falls was notorious for having one of the lowest unemployment rates in the state. Since at any given time, economists figured that one out of twenty people were switching from one job to another, they said that statistically, five percent unemployment meant everyone who wanted a job had one. Sioux Falls hovered around two percent, and local wags would often point to some guy leaning against a shovel and say, "He must be one of the three percent."

Claire knew that WorkReady wasn't going to increase her odds much, but she wanted to try an experiment. She walked in and eyed the crowd. Slack-jawed, they eyed her back.

"Hey, baby, you need some help today?" A slim pock-faced man with a greasy ponytail sidled up to her and the baby.

John eyed him then looked away. Claire followed the look. On the edge of a fiberglass bench sat an enormous Lakota Indian—Lakota because Claire figured because this was where their tribe was from, and Indian because his long black hair hung down the back of his sleeveless denim shirt. His eyes were blank and empty, his hands and arms and neck covered with crude tattoos, cuts, and scars.

Yikes, not him!

She walked toward the back of the office area, her back to the native, trying to sneak by. John had other ideas. While she was sidling by, he lurched himself forward and away from her arms. Swaying to catch her balance, she stepped sideways and into the space of the massive Lakota. Startled, he looked up in time to catch the baby in one hand with an apprehensive Claire a few inches away.

Caught in his space, awkwardly grasping for her wiggling baby, she decided to trust her instincts. "You wanna hold him while I fill out some paperwork?"

He was no longer looking at her. His eyes were instead locked in astonishment on John.

Here goes nothing. She backed away to the counter and asked for the paperwork for finding day-labor employees. It took about fifteen minutes.

When she was done, the bored, raspy-voiced attendant glanced over the papers and flicked some ash into a cup underneath a No Smoking sign. "You got anyone in particular you wanna hire?"

Claire glanced back and did a double take. The Lakota was staring into John's eyes while two streams of tears ran down his scarred cheeks. The baby was staring back at him.

"How 'bout that big guy with the baby?"

Chapter 19 - Matt Bradley

It was Matt Bradley's last formal day at KCHD-AM 1610, at least under the protective wing of Hall Media. The shoe took a while to drop in the heavily regulated broadcast world. First, there was a buzz about a possible sale of the radio section, with Hall Media dumping the whole radio floor, a rumor that had all the employees nervous and had Trent Wheeler patrolling the halls like the captain of a freighter during U-boat season.

After that, it was heard that no, just one station was being sold. There were still rumors among the jocks that South Dakota Public Broadcasting had nabbed one of the FM frequencies. Those with contacts made frantic calls from about what the pay and benefits might be for those who moved over to the public side.

And then the shoe finally dropped. KCHD was out. There was a sigh of relief all around the building. Salespeople double-checked their numbers to make sure they had no paying advertisers. More sighs of relief. "Nope, only a few bonus spots, no big deal."

Now that everybody was safe, the gossips in the building looped around to glean what they could from the sole employee of KCHD, Matt Bradley. At the news that he was to move to an undisclosed location in town to unknown owners of a station with an undisclosed format, Matt became gloomy. But since Matt was always gloomy, no one noticed.

Matt's introduction to broadcasting had been accidental. A Sioux Falls native, he was a paperboy for the *Sioux Empire Plains Beacon*, delivering papers on the north side on his bicycle, a big gloomy kid grinding his way through one hundred fifty papers a day. Each year, they'd post the pictures of the top delivery boys on the back of the Sunday paper, and each year, Matt Bradley would loom over all the other kids, big for his age, old for his age, a gloomy expression on his face. On a particular Saturday morning, Matt was picking up papers from the loading dock, along with the stacks of inserts to be stuffed into each paper before delivery, when Maynard Magnusson, the farm director for KHAL, came wheeling into the lot in a hurry.

"You, kid! Come with me!"

Matt heaved himself to his feet and lumbered after the out-of-breath Magnusson.

"I got a buncha FFA-ers coming in from the stock show, and I need you to run the board while I interview them."

If Matt was nervous, he didn't show it. Magnusson pushed through the door of the old studio and showed Matt the pots for the two guest mics and the pot for the network.

"Ride these levels, to keep them right around this black line. Turn this pot down to cue." Magnusson dialed it down until it clicked. "Hear that beeping? That's the satellite. When you hear a long beep, that'll be ten seconds before the top of the hour. Then turn the pot up to here." He pointed to about ten o'clock on the dial. "I will wrap it up in time, and the network will take over."

He dashed out of the studio to herd a bunch of nervous kids in blue corduroy into the neighboring booth. Matt did what he was asked with gloomy aplomb, and suddenly, he became a weekend board op. This led to board-opping ball games, a later decision to become a broadcast journalism major at the local Augustana College, and finally, full-time work at the Hall Media Radio Group, where he developed a reputation as a hardworking grinder who didn't complain and therefore could be given all the shit jobs.

The last shit job was program director of KCHD-AM 1620, Music of Yesteryear. That had meant producing a lot of commercials for all the stations in the group and programming all the various satellite programs into the stations' format clock, a dazzling array of car shows, religious shows, church simulcasts, infomercials, Art Bell at night, network news, local weather, and of course, Music of Yesteryear between the cracks.

But that would soon end. Trent Wheeler was the General Manager and the one who broke the news officially. "Hey, Matt, got a minute?"

Matt exhaled. "Not really. I have to ride the board in about forty-five seconds and catch a network feed." He heaved himself to his feet and started lumbering toward the studio patch bay.

Wheeler walked beside him, checking his watch. "Well, uh, I've got a sales meeting to catch myself, and I was going to head out after that, meet with some clients."

It was well known in the building that Wheeler had a weekly tee off at two o'clock each Friday afternoon, and the clients were other managers with a similar work ethic. Matt punched through the studio door, plopped down at the board, and rotated the pot controlling the network feed counter-clockwise until he felt it click into cue. Now the steady electronic *bip, bip* of the seconds could be heard counting down to the top of the hour.

"Gee, uh…" Wheeler paused. "Sorry to tell you this, but the station's been sold, and even though you've been a great asset, we're gonna have to let you go too. You're a great guy with a great future…"

Both men were looking at the sweeping second hand and listening to the *bip* of the satellite. Wheeler had about fifteen seconds left.

"Wish you the best of luck, come to me if you have any questions at all, make sure to see Diane VanDenBosch, she will have your severance check and will want your key, and don't forget I've scheduled a meat-and-cheese tray for a little going-away party for you in the break room Monday at ten—it's been great."

Fourteen seconds. Wheeler was able to clap him on the shoulder and scoot out of the studio just before the network feed.

After that, the news spread quickly. Jocks came first, bitching about the way he'd been given the boot. "Typical Wheeler-Dealer. Cold, man."

Then came the sales staff. "Matt, this is terrible! As if it's not hard enough to get a production order filled! Do you know if they are going to replace you or at least get another person in for production? Here—can you cut these specs before you leave? The client loves your voice, and you are such a professional…"

Monday came, and there was a cardboard box from Diane VanDenBosch with an exit interview scheduled for noon and a couple dozen production orders from various salespeople.

Matt sighed gloomily and headed for the production studio with the orders. He worked hard but was a little late to the break room for the going-away party—he got there at ten fifteen, but like piranhas, the other employees had come and gone, picking the food trays clean. There was a card with about ten signatures, a balloon that said Good Luck! and Trent Wheeler stuffing the last of the cheese and meat into his mouth.

"Hey! Where you been?" Trent had the decency to look a little sheepish as he pointed to an empty tray covered with crumbs and a few leaves of wilted lettuce. "I tried to make them wait, but…" He shrugged.

Matt trudged up to the third floor with his cardboard box. Diane's eyes narrowed as he walked into her office. With her glasses on the edge of her nose, she wrapped up his career at Hall Media. Severance pay for the four days worked since the last pay period. Vacation pay voided, sick pay voided, 401k plan—ineligible. His health plan was canceled as of that morning.

She looked and said pointedly, "So don't try to go to the doctor on this health plan. It will be rejected."

The fifteen-minute meeting ended with him giving her a copy of his key to the building and the contact information for the new station owners.

"I have no idea if they are interested in any existing KCHD personnel." She looked at him doubtfully then turned back to her desk. Exit interview over.

Heaving a sigh, Matt pulled himself to his feet, grabbed his cardboard box, and headed for the front door, a twenty-three-year-old has-been.

When he was halfway out of her office, Diane said, "And, Matt, just a minute."

Matt paused at the doorway.

"Is that your stapler?"

Chapter 20 - Harrison Hall

Dr. Harrison Hall IV fiddled with the paperweight, the only thing visible on the large expanse of desktop. He stared out the window, thinking through a game plan that he was not sure he had the power to implement. Deidre was dangerous. She had no scruples, and it was a mistake to have let her into the family. She simply did not know the first thing about law or strategy. He shouldn't have told her about the meeting with Meyer and the surgical staff. It was none of her business. But once she thought he was hiding something, she would not let up and could be persuasive until she'd forced out every detail.

As if she could have done any better. It wasn't like he could turn back the clock and undo the stupid blundering of his overly coddled son. The fact was, Deidre wasn't bright enough for this kind of work. She had no education to speak of, only a nursing degree from a state school. She was far beneath his station. In hindsight he could see that she'd manipulated him, using her physicality as a ploy—a tool to gain access to the powerful Hall name.

He glanced at the door. Just the thought of betraying her made him nervous. She had the uncanny cunning ability to read his mind and always seemed to be a step ahead of him—an especially irritating trait, considering her breeding.

Yet he had to admit that he could not resist her will—the way she stood and looked at him with those witch eyes that made him fearful and excited and ashamed and servile. He hated how easily she could manipulate him. That was why this kind of thinking was so dangerous and so necessary. But he had to be careful. Fortunately, she was out of town for a day or two. Something had come up, she'd said.

Just as well. It was better to have her out of the way while he made a few plans of his own.

Chapter 21 - Devon LaCroix

As far as medical-equipment sales went, Devon LaCroix had the perfect territory—at least, in his opinion. More money could be made, certainly, in larger cities like Chicago and Minneapolis, but more money meant more competition. More competition meant more bean counters calling out and asking for lower and lower costs on equipment. And lower costs meant lower profits, and lower profits meant lower commissions.

No sir, South Dakota was fine with him, with smaller hospitals with less leverage and docs happy to have a competent rep who knew his line and knew how to help implement it. It did mean a lot of time on the road, but in truth, Devon liked the empty road time. It was a time to drive and unwind, see the rolling plains unravel in front of the windshield—a time to be alone with his thoughts and just plain be alone.

Devon liked his freedom. He knew he was attractive to women, and he was certainly okay with the life he lived, and occasionally, his life was far more than merely okay. Like the motorcycle case he'd just had with Dr. Cooper. Some kid on a Kawasaki had been T-boned by an old lady in a minivan. LaCroix raced up to Aberdeen with a complete set and got it there in time to get it into the autoclave for sterilization and an early-morning surgery. Eight hours, four plates, thirty-six screws, a hip, and a hip socket.

That kid will set off metal detectors for the rest of his life. Devon whistled tunelessly while he calculated his commission on the hardware. It had been a long and satisfying day.

He was enjoying a Twins game at the Ramada Inn bar when he noticed the very thing that could make a great day end even better. She was sitting at the end of the bar, in some kind of scrubs—shapeless blue and drab but not so shapeless that he did not notice the curves underneath. *Hello!* He casually sat near but not next to her. It was his lucky decision to have kept his scrubs on as well. *Common ground.*

"Hey. How goes the battle?"

She puffed out her cheeks and exhaled. "Long and intense. Still waiting on the casualty report." She lifted what looked like a Bloody Mary. "To blood and guts."

He hoisted his beer. "*Semper Fi.*"

She laughed. "Oh, no! Not a jarhead!"

Devon's eye twinkled. "Not at first. Took a tour as a Navy corpsman, then re-enlisted as one of the few and the proud." He took a sip and appraised her. "Don't tell me...Navy?"

She rolled her eyes. "Oh, don't even try. I spent four years fending off full-on assaults from better than you, buddy boy."

He held up his hands. "All right, I surrender. I just came out of a full day in surgery and am tapped already. Truce?"

She raised her glass slightly. "Truce." She leveled a gaze with a twinkle in her eyes that sent a thrill up LaCroix's spine.

To hell with a truce. The battle is just beginning. He gave his predatory grin and motioned to the stool next to her. "Permission to come alongside?"

Her smile curved, and her voice dipped a notch. "Permission granted."

He quickly checked for rings. None. He reached to flip over her name tag, a practiced move that worked well. "So… nice to meet you, Nurse D. Keckley."

She gave a long and throaty laugh full of promise. Her eyes were sea green and hungry. "Why don't you call me Deidre?"

Chapter 22 - Stan Martin

Stan Martin stood in the middle of what was supposed to be a radio station and sighed. The squall from the morning was over, but puddles of melted snow and mud were tracked up and down the hallway—inconsequential really, but the added mess depressed him.

There were tons of things to be done. He could see that by looking at the boxes of equipment, rolls of wiring, stacks of drywall, and general disarray. He was not a jack-of-all-trades. He was a jack of one trade. He had a gift for finding news, researching news, writing news, and reporting news. He had no gift at all for mechanical things or for using mechanical things to build things.

But at the very least, he could recognize competency when he saw it, and Claire's cousins Wes and Cal had it in spades. They had boundless energy. Although they had a place to sleep at Stan and Claire's apartment, they were hardly ever there. They spent seemingly twenty-four hours a day at the station, moving walls, hauling drywall, and unloading equipment. The dust and noise was ever present, but progress was noticeable.

"Hey, guys, you want something to eat?" Stan had stopped at a drive-through and bought a selection of sandwiches.

Cal stopped immediately. "Yep." Thirty seconds later, Wes appeared from a back room as if in answer to an invisible summons and grabbed a burger in a wrapper.

Both sat down on what was available, Cal on a five-gallon bucket of drywall compound and Wes on a box of wire. In unison, both dropped their heads for fifteen seconds. Then Cal said "Amen," and they started eating the same way they worked, steadily and with a minimum of talking.

"How's it going?" Stan asked.

"Good," Wes said around some food. Cal nodded.

Great conversation. Stan looked around at the state of construction.

After the brothers were hired, he'd sat down with them and sketched out what he wanted on a piece of paper—small reception area, two production studios, main broadcast studio, and an open area for desks. Cal and Wes nodded.

"Can you do this?" Stan asked.

"Yep," Cal said.

"Any questions?"

Wes thought. "Nope."

Cal added, "Not yet."

Wes had nodded.

Now it was mid-March, and the clock was ticking.

"I want to be up and running, get my staff by the first of the April. It doesn't have to be pretty, but it does have to work. Can you do it?" Stan asked.

Cal and Wes stopped chewing. Both stared off into space with intense concentration for a solid minute.

Wes spoke first. "Yep."

Cal looked at Wes like he was checking his calculations. Then he, too, nodded. "Yep."

Stan looked at both of them, wanting to ask about certain aspects of the work, confirm specs, go over timelines. They looked back at him while they ate. Each crumpled up their wrapper and tossed it into an empty cardboard box in the corner, and they each picked up another sandwich simultaneously.

Stan shrugged. "Okay." He stood up from a dusty folding chair and clapped the drywall dust off his pants. "Any questions for me?"

Cal and Wes were reaching for the cups of soda. "Nope," they answered in the same way at the same time. They'd done it often enough that it no longer surprised Stan.

"Okay, then. I'm going to start looking for employees."

Stan turned in time to see a large man with a cardboard box standing in the doorway. He was dressed in baggy khakis and a wrinkled dress shirt with a tail hanging out the back. His glasses were smudged, and one of his tennis shoes was untied. He leaned his bulk against the doorframe for support. He had large forearms, a world-weary expression, and a mess of black hair liberally shot with gray.

"Can I help you?" As Stan approached him, he realized that the man was not in his midfifties or his midforties. No, to his astonishment, he realized this was probably a college kid.

The kid heaved a sigh, setting the cardboard box of office supplies on the floor. He stood up and, in a practiced gesture, ran his hands around his waistband, tucking the shirttail in and hoisting the khakis up a few inches. Then he adjusted his glasses and leaned back against the doorframe. "Yeah, maybe. I was told this was the place where the new radio station is going to be." He consulted a piece of paper off the top of the cardboard box. "You know if Emilio Gonzales is here?"

Stan appraised him. "Not now, he's not. How may I help you?"

The kid fished another piece of paper off the top of the box, smoothed it on his pants, and handed it to Stan. "My name's Matt Bradley." He said it like he was admitting to some small crime. "I was program director at KCHD."

Stan scanned the résumé while the kid heaved a sigh and settled into the doorframe. "You're from here?"

The kid looked like he might as well admit it. "Yeah. I grew up on the North Side."

"It says here you worked for B&C Incorporated while you were in High School. What's that?"

"Yeah, but I also worked for Hall Media group then. I was in distribution." He pointed to another line on the résumé.

Stan guessed. "Paper boy?"

The kid sighed again like it was useless to defend himself. "Yeah. Ten years."

"And B&C?"

"That was working summers for my dad. He's the B. My mom's the C."

"Doing what?"

"Construction. Framing and drywall mainly. Sometimes electrical."

Stan shook Matt's large, dry, lifeless hand. It was like shaking an empty catcher's mitt. "I've got to get some paperwork. Contract, tax stuff, pay period, things like that. This is a start-up, and we're building it as we go. There's two cowboys in back called Wes and Cal. Ask them what you can do to help. Tie your shoe—it's loose—and I'll be back in about an hour."

Heaving a sigh, the kid tied his shoe and went in search of his first assignment.

Chapter 23 - Charlie Hofer

At first, Charlie Hofer's plan for vengeance was just an idea. He'd gotten a hold of Stan Martin on a whim. He knew Stan Martin's name, of course, because of the murders out in the western part of the state. South Dakota was seldom in the national spotlight, so the story out of Dansing, South Dakota, got more airplay in the state than elsewhere, and Stan Martin was almost a household name because of it.

He was, in fact, a little surprised that he was able to find him and present him with a job and that Martin actually took it. *Money talks*. Hofer was also surprised at how little radio announcers made. He was prepared to pay much more to get his pound of flesh and had been pleasantly surprised at how fast and cheap this Martin guy was getting the job done.

Now they were starting to wrap things up. With just a few more meetings, Hofer would be able to sit back and watch his creation come alive. Martin was in his office for his weekly meeting. Both Hofer and Martin agreed that keeping Hofer in the background for as long as possible was the best play. Martin had a few schematics for the meeting and some Polaroids of the progress done as well as written cost estimates and timelines.

Hofer snapped his fingers. "Hey!" He looked at Martin and rolled his eyes. "Hey! Bitch!"

Veronica called from down the hall, "I'm coming, I'm com... ohh!" She came into the room and looked at Martin, surprised. One hand flew to her hair, and the other smoothed her dress. "Hey, Stan."

Stan had half stood. "Good morning, Mrs. Hofer."

Hofer was irritated. "Sit down, Martin. She ain't no frickin' queen of England." He turned to his wife. "What I tell ya? I got meetings in my office. I wanna entertain some people, an' I got no ice."

Veronica responded to Hofer, but her eyes were on Martin. "Sure, Charlie. Comin' right up." She touched Martin on the shoulder. "Can I get you anything, Stan?"

"No, but thank you for asking."

Hofer rolled his eyes again. *Guy acts like James Bond.* "Let's cut to the chase." He motioned to the papers in front of him.

Stan leaned forward. "Okay. Two of the walls have been moved. The drywall is up and mudded, ready to be textured. Wires are all pulled, and the boards are in, ready to be installed. We decided not to use the board from Hall Media. It was an old Gates model, hard to get parts for and a little long in the tooth. Plus, we didn't want to show up and run the risk of staff members asking questions. One of the techs found out about a station in Alaska going bankrupt and got some pretty good used stuff—tape deck, cart desks, automation system—should be coming in tomorrow right after the painting is done. The transmitter is ancient—we're talking tubes out of World War II. I guess the previous owners bought it all up as surplus at pennies on the dollar. My engineers say there're enough tubes and parts to build ten transmitters, so we might as well keep it."

Hofer looked at the Polaroids and ignored the schematics and the technical talk. *Whatever.* "So, this place gonna be done on time?"

"First of the month," Martin said.

"And the name?"

This had caused a little argument. Hofer had wanted to put his mark on the call letters and wanted the assholes at the Oaks to know where their pain was coming from. "How 'bout FYOU?"

"Can't. FCC regulations dictate anything west of the Mississippi must begin with a K."

Hofer leered. "Okay, then, backward—KCUF."

"Taken."

Hofer pouted. "By who?"

"Hard rock station in California."

Hofer tried again. "KUNT? KOCK?" Martin looked at him for a long minute until Hofer looked away. "Okay, okay." He thought again. "How 'bout Karma?"

Martin nodded. "Better, but that's taken too. Station out of Denver, KRMA." Then he added, "Just got FCC approval yesterday. But KCAH—with your initials—is all yours."

KCAH-AM 1620, the Voice of Truth. It wasn't edgy enough for his taste, but Hofer could see how it might carry some weight with the other media in town. And it did sound legit, which was probably good too.

The first of April, KCAH would take to the airwaves, and Charles Alvin Hofer would use his station to crucify the mealy-mouthed pricks that dared look down at him.

Chapter 24 - Stan Martin

Stan stood next to the transmitter shack, looked up at the KCAH tower site, and got a queasy feeling. Tall and spindly, the red-and-white tower looked just like the thousands of others that dotted the landscape— harmless and almost invisible until you got close to it. *Yikes*.

Craning his neck, he could see Cal about halfway up. The KCAH tower was only four hundred feet tall. On paper, that seemed a mundane number. But standing next to it, craning his neck to look up at it, Stan felt his skin crawl. Hazard signs everywhere, shouting DANGER and HIGH VOLTAGE, and WARNING, weren't helping.

He turned to Wes. "What's he doing up there?"

Wes seemed unconcerned. "Climbing it."

Stan studied him to see if he was being a smartass. Apparently not. "But why exactly is he climbing it?"

"Inspection." Then in a rare burst of words, Wes said, "Towers are tricky. They need to be maintained to make sure they don't fall. This one's a pair of two-hundred-footers spliced together. Cal's making sure it's good is all."

No big deal. Just like climbing a ladder with four hundred rungs. Stan shuddered. He'd climbed the side of an elevator once, not nearly as high and a lot more stable, and the memory of that was bad enough.

"How's the signal?"

"Dunno." After a fifteen-second pause, Wes said, "Checking the structure first. Then we'll power it up and see."

Stan motioned to the HIGH VOLTAGE sign. "What's going to be hot when the power goes on?"

Now it was Wes's turn to look at Stan, seeing if he was joking. Stan shrugged. The mechanics of how things worked had never been his strong suit, especially the mysteries of radio transmission.

Wes explained. "This whole tower's gonna be hot. Top to bottom. Not like an FM tower, where you carry the transmitter to the top. In AM, the tower *is* the transmitter, like a big tuning fork." Wes pointed to gray bulges in the guy wires, three sets of them spaced out on each wire. "Them insulators are called Johnny balls. They keep the charge from hitting the ground. You see them on a tower, you can definitely tell it's an AM tower." Then he pointed to a large amber rod at the base of the tower. "That's insulated too. Solid glass. Keeps the electricity from reaching the ground. If this tower is on, and you touch it, you will be messed up. So you jump from the ice shield."

Stan looked at the latticed-steel framework over the building that led out over the bundles of electrical cable like a heavy-duty dock. "Ice shield?"

"Yep. When you get freezing rain on this tower, and the wind starts blowing or the temperature rises, huge chunks of ice fall down like shrapnel." Wes pointed to the end of the ice shield. "You stand on the edge of the dock-looking thing, and you jump, like leapfrog. Never step over."

Stan studied it and cringed. "Like a bug zapper?"

Wes shrugged. "Not sure. Depends on the wattage. It's not like regular electricity—it's RF burns. It hurts long and deep and strange, kinda like being in a microwave. Parts of you get cooked."

Stan thought about being in a microwave and shuddered. "But Cal's off the ground, like a bird on a power line."

Wes shrugged again. "Probably. Weird, though. Kinda like sound—sometimes the wires will pick up the frequency and zap you a bit."

Zap you a bit. Stan felt his skin crawl.

Wes needled him. "How'd you like to be in the weather ball?"

Stan stared up four hundred feet at the small booth at the top of the tower and shuddered again. *Not in a million years.*

***

It had been a great promotion, best of the best. Sioux Empire National Bank had figured out a way to hook its name with the obsession of every South Dakotan and potential customer—the weather ball.

At the top of the bank building was a small tower that would change along with a heavily promoted ditty:

When the weather ball is glowing red, warmer weather is just ahead.

When the weather ball is shining white, colder weather is in sight.

When the weather ball is wearing green, no weather changes are foreseen.

Colors blinking by night and day say precipitation's on the way.

Back in the day, the station manager of KCSC-AM 1620—King Corn Seed Company—had gotten the bank to pay for a weather ball at the top of the radio tower so it could be seen by farmers in the area. A small booth was placed there to shield the apparatus from moisture, but it kept failing anyway. Eventually, the bank lost interest, and the station was sold. The weather ball had stayed broken at the top of the tower, too expensive to fix or dismantle, a forgotten piece of Sioux Falls history.

Chapter 25 - Deidre Hall

Before she married the weak and wealthy Harrison Benjamin Hall IV, Deidre Hall knew she was bound for greatness. From a very young age, the girl then known as Deidre Keckley was aware that she was different. She hid it well, of course. She learned how to perform behaviors and emotions that others expected, and when she got older, she found that she could use her sexuality to easily mask her different nature.

The fact of the matter was that people disgusted her. They were so stupid. So easily manipulated. Controlling people was what life was about—a chance to move and maneuver, to take and build and control. As a young girl, she was fascinated to see what was inside things—to figure out what made them feel pain and how long they could withstand it.

Once her teacher caught her poking a stick into a cat's eye by the edge of the schoolyard. Seeing the horrified look in her eyes, Deidre quickly burst into tears and sobbed uncontrollably, mumbling about a neighbor man who'd touched her and made her feel ashamed. The stupid cunt believed her, holding her close and telling her it would be all right. It *was* all right after a while. If she had to do it all over again, she would have thought of a different lie. She'd pointed out an elderly neighbor, a retired postman named John, and by sticking to her lie and sobbing and shuddering and shaking her head and shivering, she was able to make them believe her. There was no evidence, but there were a lot of angry neighbors, and one day John the postman was beaten up badly, and he moved away. Crisis averted.

After that, she was much more careful. She excelled in biology, pretending to be squeamish at the dissection labs, then moved on to college and a nursing degree. She didn't have the mind for all the memorization a doctor's degree required, but she also didn't have the patience or see the need. As a nurse, she'd been able to study the doctors up close until she could select the one who would be most useful to her.

Now Deidre Hall had a name that gave her instant access to power and secrets and invulnerability. Stupid little Benjy had almost taken that away from her—almost destroyed the Hall name—but fortunately, she'd been able to discover the problem and take care of it. In her observation, men were either goats or sheep.

When she first saw Devon LaCroix in the bar, she immediately knew he was a goat—a stupid sex-driven goat—and from there it was easy. She got him to take her to her hotel room and agree to a mutual shower and a little choking as a way to increase stimulus. And as he was erect and inside her, thrusting away, she choked him... and *poof*, he collapsed, dazed and unresponsive. Fortunately, he was in the shower. She quickly rolled him on his back, grabbed the scalpel that was waiting next to the sink, and poked it deep into his carotid. Riding his convulsing corpse, she climaxed. Then, waiting a full twenty minutes for the blood to drain away with the hot water gave her time to compose herself, get the garbage bags, and get to work.

It was pretty simple really—not much different from cutting up a chicken. With a sharp scalpel for the tendons and a knowledge of joints and anatomy, *snik-snak*, she finished up. Ninety minutes later, she was showered with her hair done and makeup applied, and two heavy suitcases were waiting by the door.

Chapter 26 - Oscar Holmberg

Oscar Holmberg was a junior at Northern State, working his way through school, doing odd hours at the Ramada. The call came at eleven o'clock at night. *Weird that somebody checks out at night, but oh well.* The chick wore dark glasses, had a big handbag almost like a shopping bag, and carried two huge Samsonite suitcases. *Mother of God, they're heavy!* Fortunately they had those little wheels on the bottom, but even so, one of them flopped over as he pulled it into the elevator, and it was a bitch setting the thing upright.

Then he brought them out to her car, and *shit*, he had to hoist those bad boys into the trunk of her rental car. There was plenty of room in the trunk. *Geez, you could toss a body in here!* But even so, the thing sagged a bit.

Oscar wiped the sweat off his brow, because his brow was sweaty and because that was a good way to get a little extra tip money. "There ya go, lady. So whaddaya got in there, a side of beef?"

She flickered a smile, gave him a fiver, and drove away.

Chapter 27 - Claire

It turned out the Lakota was named John, too, just like her son. John Returns From Hunt. He was born into the Sicangu Lakota Reservation, out by Rosebud, and had lived a life of trouble and turmoil.

He did not talk much at first. He would show up at the start of the day and ask to hold her baby. It scared the hell out of Stan. She'd told him about the hire but not in a lot of detail, so when he headed out to the Shark—his name for his trusty old Chrysler 300—he was surprised to see this enormous Indian with scars and tattoos hanging out in the parking lot by Claire's truck. Stan had a recent history with scary-looking guys who'd almost killed him, so he was a little gun-shy.

Fortunately, Claire was right behind him on the way to her old jobsite. Introductions were made and apologies accepted. Stan then looked at Claire with that penetrating look he was known for. She was holding baby John.

Once Stan had driven away, the Indian asked, "Can I hold your baby?"

Claire shrugged and handed him off. From then on, she started calling them Big John and Little John.

Their mornings would start at about five thirty. Claire would make a pot of coffee, scramble some eggs with toast or something similar—fast-order stuff she could whip up in a hurry, a relic from her waitress days. Stan would come back from a run about six o'clock. By then, Big John would be there, crowding in the kitchen if the weather was bad or, on warm days, sitting outside on their stoop, drinking coffee, eating, watching the weather, and waiting.

After Stan showered, shaved, and got dressed, he would slide into the table, finish his breakfast, and play with Little John a bit, talking morning talk with Claire. Then he'd kiss the baby, hand him off to Big John on the stoop, and head off to work. A moment after that, Claire would appear outside with a refresher for Big John's mug and a mug of her own. They would sit together on the stoop and plan the day, Little John staring in Big John's eyes and Big John staring back.

While she drank her coffee, Claire would watch the two of them out of the corner of her eye. She wasn't sure what was happening. The look they shared seemed so personal that she felt like she was intruding on some hidden conversation that was none of her business. When the look was done, Big John would sigh deeply, exhaling something from within. Then, eyes down, he would look gently in her direction, ready for the day's work.

That day, it was the concrete work. Claire had sent Big John off to get his driver's license, a necessity she was willing to pay for, and was expecting a contractor to bid on a foundation that house would be moved to. She had the permits the city needed and had the plot staked out with slats of wood topped with pink plastic streamers.

She was eying the property, with Little John in her arms, when the guy from Top Notch pulled in. "Mornin'!"

He had a new truck and wore a striped work shirt rolled up to the biceps with the name Sonny sewed onto the patch over his shirt pocket.

"Mornin'!" Claire stepped up while Sonny looked around. "Anyone here?"

"Yeah, I am."

It was an aggravation but one Claire was getting used to. Perplexed men at the city office, perplexed men at the jobsite, perplexed men at the lumberyard, all wondering where the man was.

Sonny rolled his Oakleys back off his face and perched them upside down on the back of his head. He was in shape and knew it. He put his hands on his hips, looking down at her. "So you the one in charge?" The sentence amused him.

Rather than get into that, Claire motioned to the ground in front of her. "I want a basement, nine feet deep, about five feet below grade. I figure I'll have the dirt work graded up the side at about ten degrees so it'll cover up most of the foundation in front and give me a walk-out on the back facing the alley."

Sonny was watching her talk. His eyes had done a slow appraisal from her shoes on up. Apparently, he was impressed. "This'll work out great!" He was fiddling with the ring on his finger.

Claire was pretty certain by that point but wanted to make sure. "Here." She handed the baby over to him—or tried to.

Little John squirmed and fought and scowled. Sonny looked nonplussed. "What do you want me to do?" He looked doubtfully at the silent but squirming baby.

Claire nodded. *Suspicions confirmed.* "I want you to leave and not bother coming back."

Claire spun on her heel and headed inside to set an appointment for the next contractor.

Chapter 28 - Harrison Hall

Dr. Harrison Hall kept a light but constant surgical schedule—about two surgeries a week, enough to keep his hand in, stay up-to-date with the constant evolution of medicine, and know he hated it. Well, maybe not hate. The surgery was okay. It was the constant nattering of the patients, like bleating sheep before the slaughter, that he didn't like.

"Is this going to hurt?"

"How long will it take to recover?"

"What will this cost?"

And the staff members were almost worse—the leery ones who recognized his name and avoided eye contact as well as the sycophantic ones who hung on his every word, laughing like jackasses at the right moment. He hated the glances between the nurses, the unheard conversation, the judging and comparing.

And the very worst of all were the salespeople. The hallways were littered with pharmaceutical sales reps with their constant free lunches and seminars. There were hospital-bed salespeople, lab-equipment salespeople, software and hardware reps and those who sold x-ray, temperature, ultrasound, and CAT scan machines … all patrolling the halls like sharks, wearing hungry, savage smiles, looking to rip out a pound of profits.

It was much safer in his office. There he could protect himself with layers of gatekeepers and soundproof doors and calm receptionists to chase them away. *But*… but the one time he could have used a competent person to quickly explain the ins and outs of a certain device without having to wade through insipid instruction videos or pamphlets in twelve languages and impossible jargon…

He glared at the nurse and the rest of the surgical team. "So where is the Panco rep?"

Silence. Finally, a nurse spoke up. "She's driving up from Omaha. She was in surgery early this morning and was going to get here as soon as she could."

Hall was irate. "Omaha! Don't we have our own rep?"

"Yes, we do. Devon LaCroix. He's usually right on time. But I guess he's sick or something. No one can find him. He drove up to Aberdeen for a hip surgery, and now he's nowhere."

At the sound of Devon LaCroix's name, small shrill alarms started going off in the back of Hall's mind, pushing the irritations of surgery into insignificance. A cold chill ran down his spine.

Chapter 29 - Don Keshane

Don Keshane knew how to hustle, and hustling was what he did best. He started out hustling as a kid outside the Arkota Ballroom in Sioux Falls, shining shoes—a nickel a shine—back when he was Donnie Ten Bom. He'd say "A nickel a shine" then try to double it to a nickel a shoe. Half the time it worked. Sometimes it would even get him a tip. A smartass kid asking for double—folks liked his moxie.

When he was thirteen, he saw the end of the big bands and the beginning of rock 'n' roll. He had no voice for singing, but he realized that the guys who could sing only did it to score chicks, and the ballrooms only booked kids to sell tickets, and there was plenty of margin in the middle for a smart-talking manager.

He made some good hay doing that, booking Legion halls for a few bucks, paying the guys in the acts free beer and girls, paying himself a big fat slice of everything that was left. At the peak, he was putting aside a good five hundred bucks a week in cash, tax-free. Taking his big mouth to the local radio station, KHAL—a big stick that broadcast to three hundred miles of bored teenagers stuck on farms and small towns—Donnie talked his way into doing an air shift between ten at night and one in the morning, a dead time for most adults and prime time for teenagers. He called it the Sock Hop, convinced them to pay him thirty percent of the proceeds from any ads sold, and let him pick the music.

He did that for four years, changed his name to Don Keshane—after the Wayne Newton song—and worked his mouth talking fast, playing the records that promoted local groups, and selling ads to malt shops within the huge radius of the KHAL signal. He became a celebrity and found out that chicks dug his fast patter and the fame that stuck with him. Labels called him up and offered to pay him even more money to push their music. Life was amazing. He had a closet full of suits to fit his skinny frame and a fin-tail Caddy to fit his entourage of admiring girls. It was a sweet ride before someone made up the word *payola*, and the feds got the idea that it was wrong to take money from record labels to play music. It was a good thing for Donnie that the scandal hit the big guys on the coast first and that he was still seventeen, a minor. He escaped with a hefty fine, a slap on the wrist, a repo on the Caddy, and exactly one sharkskin suit left to his name.

But he still had his mouth and his motor, and the new and improved Don Keshane bounced straight into radio sales for KHAL. He hustled and talked and peddled spots for the radio side. He tried to get over to print and TV, but the sales managers were leery, so he stuck with radio. As the number of radio stations at Hall Media grew, so did the inventory, and so did Don Keshane. Fingers snapping, gum snapping, *go, go, go*, he was all over town, always in a new Caddy—white with red trim—and always pushing and talking and selling then back to the stations and talking to the jocks, wheedling a spec ad for a special client, or hanging around the studio, checking the on-air log. He got caught writing in free ads for the morning show log on KCHD-FM, which was called HITZ 103. The general manager, Troy Wheeler, busted him, and Don talked his way out of it, saying he just sold a last-minute annual buy with a flight of bonus ads, and since the logs were already printed, he was just writing them in. Wheeler shrugged because he really didn't care, but that bookkeeping bitch Diane VanDenBosch did, and the next time Donnie did it, he was canned—tossed out with no thank-you or reference letter, not allowed to return to the property under any circumstances.

"Screw this." he decided. He took a plane to Vegas, spent two weeks and twenty grand—ten of his own, ten on a credit card. Then he limped home and knocked on the door of Hall Media, new carnation in his lapel, a jaunty snap-brim hat in hand… the new humble Don Keshane.

A security cop met him at the door and, resisting all patter, shoved him back onto the street.

"You will rue the day you messed with Don Keshane!" he shouted at the closed door as shocked and satisfied former coworkers smirked at his downfall through the glass walls of the front lobby.

Assholes!

Pride wounded to the core, Don Keshane shot the cuffs on his sharkskin suit and walked stiffly to his Caddy. *They will rue the day.* He didn't know what *rue* meant, but he'd heard that in a movie once, and it sounded good.

He squealed out of the lot and found himself heading south on Minnesota past a couple of car dealerships, thinking about the car biz. Hungry, he hung a left on Twenty-Sixth Street. There was a Chinese buffet that he still had some freebie coupons to—radio giveaways. The long habit of trolling for new clients was still in place. His eyes darted left and right, looking for new signs. Without even thinking, he slowed when he saw the new sign on the corner of Twenty-Sixth and Cleveland: KCAH-AM 1620, the Voice of Truth.

He almost stopped in traffic. *Hello.*

Chapter 30 - Veronica Hofer

Veronica Hofer—formerly Doris Tschetter—was a farm girl, fifth of ten children from Centerville, South Dakota. Now known as the Goody Gal, she was the common-law wife of Charlie Hofer. Veronica looked curiously at Stan Martin.

Charlie had been dismissive. "An alky. Can't hold his booze." Charlie had nothing nice to say about anybody, and with Stan—the guy who was running his radio station—he was no different. To prove his superiority, he'd sloshed some Scotch in a tumbler and tossed it down. "Will say, though, I hired the right guy. He's doing everything I want on time and under budget."

That was like Charlie—turning a compliment about someone else into a compliment about himself. Doris—as she still thought herself—had a long and storied past with Charlie. She'd met him while working at the Shell station off of Highway 16.

Her dad was an alcoholic himself and had told all the kids, "Have a plan, because when you're eighteen, you're out."

Doris did not have a plan. She couldn't think of what to do, and the next week was her eighteenth birthday. She knew Charlie Hofer by sight. He had a strip club off the interstate south of Beresford—kind of a creepy guy, never looked her in the face, always eyed her up and down. But at least he looked at her like she was worth something, even if she was just a body to ogle.

"You ever need a job?" he asked one day, tossing a twenty on the counter.

She was cautious. "Doin' what?"

"Waitressing. Serve drinks, good tips, sometimes a hunnerd a night."

She was tempted. She said she might be interested. And that was the first in a long string of lies Charlie told her. The first lie was about the waitressing. It turned out it was a topless bar. The waitress tips were given to the house and a small portion given back. Then it was mandatory that she strip if she wanted to keep her job. After that, it was presented that if she got a boob job, she'd be getting bigger tips. She gave in. Why not? Her family had already disowned her, and the town had as well, although she wound up seeing most of the men who'd shunned her down below on Friday and Saturday nights, with leers and dollar bills.

So there she was, first Miss Goody, now Mrs. Charlie Hofer. A roof over her head and a certain amount of security. *Oh well.*

Now Charlie was talking to Stan Martin in his office, and she wondered if Stan was going to wind up another victim to Charlie's lies.

"Hey!" Charlie was snapping his fingers and shouting. "Ice."

Like he can't reach the ice himself. Heaving a sigh, she walked into the office from down the hall. He just liked to watch her bend over and put it in glass. A lot of times, he would grab her boobs and ask about his investment. *His investment and my aching back, hauling these melons around, enduring the stares of others. Oh well.*

Not Stan Martin, though. He was a real gentleman, a rarity in her world. Ironically, she'd spent most of her adult life working in gentlemen's clubs and never met a gentleman. It bothered Charlie that Stan treated her nice, enough so that he treated her extra mean whenever Stan was around. It looked a few times like Stan wanted to clock Charlie for being such a jerk. His hand would flinch and fidget, making a fist. Charlie seemed not to notice.

"So it's about ready, then—KCAH?"

Stan shifted in his seat then nodded. "We'll start up Monday morning. I've hired four announcers to start, all with various duties around the station but all with news-reporting duties as well. I'm interviewing a traffic person for logs and billing, but I want to be clear—I'm not sure how much revenue we'll be getting at the beginning. For that reason, I'm about ready to hire one salesperson—straight commission, thirty percent."

Charlie waved his hand dismissively. "When you gonna start digging?" He leaned forward, eager for blood.

"On Monday. Investigative news will be part of our pedigree, but I wouldn't expect immediate results. All I can promise you is about twenty hours a week of research if we find something worthwhile—"

"But remember." Stan held his hand up for attention and focused in on Charlie. Doris admired the way he could stop Charlie in his tracks with that look he had. "I am the station news director and general manager. That means I am the only one who directs who we investigate and how much time I will devote to each story. I will not put up with any meddling or interference of any kind. If I get any of that, I will quit. Do you understand?" The voice was quiet, but the command was there, like the way guys talked in those war movies that Doris sometimes watched on TV.

Subdued, Charlie nodded, then he rallied and asked offhandedly, "You gonna need a receptionist or secretary or somethin'?"

Stan nodded. "I think so. I have the office set up for a desk in front. I expect that eventually, there will be some gatekeeping required, some way to handle phone traffic, maybe some typing."

"What about her?" Charlie jerked a thumb at Doris, startling both her and Stan.

"Me?" Doris was absolutely thunderstruck.

Stan looked to see if Charlie was joking. After a pause, he said carefully, "Well…"

Charlie barged in, "She's got plenty of experience. Too much experience. That's why I'm gettin' rid of her. You." He turned and pointed to Doris.

Doris opened and shut her mouth, staring at him.

Charlie shrugged. "It's business, baby." He hadn't called her baby in fifteen years. "Forty is about it. After that, profits *sag*." He smiled with the pun. "I thought I might try a ploy with you to get in that Oaks place, you know, with a legit older woman, not a kid, but that didn't work, and I've been lookin' for a time and a place to cut bait. This is it." He pointed to Stan. "Start workin' for him."

Completely destroyed, Doris tried to rally. "I want… a divorce."

"Hah!" barked Charlie. "Never were married, just the ring." He pointed. "You can keep it. It's zircon."

His expression was small and triumphant. He was so cruel, like he was staging this just to humiliate her in front of one of the only nice men she'd ever met.

If Stan's hand was forced, he didn't show it. He stood and looked down at Charlie. "I will not see you at the station. If I do, I will throw you out. If you must speak to me, you will call our receptionist, Miss…?" He looked at Doris.

"Tschetter. Doris Tschetter."

"Congratulations, Miss Tschetter. This is the happiest day of your life." He looked courage into her eyes then held the door open for her.

She walked out with her chin high. Doris had a feeling Stan was right. She was forty years old. Maybe this *was* the best day of her life.

Chapter 31 - Stan Martin

Stan Martin had worked in radio for most of his adult life. He understood the needs of a radio station and the needs of business. The station he was in charge of was not a business per se—it was a vendetta. But the person sitting across from him could help change that.

Could was the operative word. Since his first meeting with the man, Stan had done a little research and prepared for this, the second interview. He looked up from a résumé filled with spelling errors and focused on the twitchy man in the loud suit.

"Don Keshane?"

"You're welcome!" The guy popped four finger snaps in a row, clapped his palms together, and pointed. "Get it?"

Stan repressed a sigh. *Danke schoen* was German for "Thank you." He wondered how many times this strange, nervous man had used that line.

"You like the name?"

"It's fine. Just wondering if you used that just on the radio or to sell too." Stan's real last name was

McGarvey—most people in radio did not use their real names. But *Don Keshane* seemed a little much.

"It's got..." Again with the snapping fingers. "Style. No one ever forgets me."

Stan raised an eyebrow. "I'll bet."

Then the guy started talking. Leaning back, moving his hands, he started painting a picture of his life. The more he talked, the more the fake mannerisms were replaced with real intensity and emotion. He stood and started pacing back and forth when he got to the part about getting fired from Hall Media "for no good reason!"

Stan was nodding his head in appreciation. This strange little man was a spellbinder. Stan held up a hand to stop the flow of words. "Sit down, Donnie."

Donnie sat.

"Here's the deal, Donnie, and you probably know most of this already. It's not that big of a town. First..." Stan had a habit of ticking things off on his fingers as a way to keep things brief. "First, this is an eight-hundred-watt AM standalone station with a signal that barely reaches the edge of town. Second, it is the hobby of the month for Mr. Charlie Hofer, owner of the Goodies strip clubs. Why he has an interest in investigative journalism is probably personal, vengeful, and beyond me. Third, he has paid top dollar to build a group of reporters that can deliver on the hobby. KCAH is no paper tiger. We can and will deliver a level of news reporting that this region has never seen before. Fourth, this start-up is nothing special to look at"—Stan's gesture took in the questionable decor—"because we are very top-heavy on salaries. Fifth, there is money to be made selling this station, and I need one, just one salesperson to sell it, and that person could be you."

Donnie sat up straight, done with the BS. The deal was about to be hashed out. Stan slid a small stack of paper across the table. "Here is a program log for the last week, showing the minutes of available spots each week. If three-quarters of the spot load is sold, and all expenses are paid, this is what each spot has to sell for."

Donnie craned to look. His eyes narrowed. "Kinda steep for the market."

"Not as steep as it's going to be." Stan pointed to another figure, thirty percent higher. "See this number? That is now your spot rate. Anything you sell at this or above gets you a thirty percent commission."

Donnie's eyes glowed with predatory glee.

"Anything below that rate pays nothing."

The gleam went out. "No way."

"And you will run every proposal past Doris at the front desk."

The gleam came back. "The chick at the front door?"

Donnie started to say something, but Stan cut him off again. "Truth? Yes, she was a stripper. Yes, she is in fact a former Goodie Girl. Yes, she was married to Charlie Hofer, and yes, she has a very personal reason for making sure that every dollar is accounted for, every expense approved, and believe me when I say there is not a trick in the book that she hasn't seen before. And…" Stan leveled his gaze at Donnie until his expression sobered. "She will be treated with respect."

Subdued but not beaten, Donnie started in on his side. "That spot rate is steep for radio and impossible for this crappy signal. The Hall boys are bastards and will start running you down all over town. Charlie Hofer is a known sleazebag, and they will make sure everyone knows about who really owns this place. I'll be lucky to get a third of this rate—"

"And yet you will do it." Stan's statement stopped Donnie cold. "Donnie, here's the deal. I know a salesperson when I see one. I also see how you have created niches and markets where none existed before. You have spent a lifetime being fast and devious. And you will spend the rest of your life being fast and ethical. It is time to lose the shiny suit and dress like the professional you really are. The first thing you will do is get a trade out for two thousand dollars' worth of good suits at Norman's. The second thing you will do is figure out how you're going to sell this station, the rate card, the packages, the pitch—the works. And the last thing you will do is accomplish the very thing that made you stop here instead of going to sell cars or office machines or furniture or houses." Stan leaned forward and closed the deal—selling the salesman, beating him at his own game. "You will have your vengeance."

Chapter 32 - Claire

Claire pulled into the parking lot of the radio station. She was on the way to pick up some lumber at the yard downtown, but it was the first week of the station being open, and she was curious to see what had happened in the last few weeks.

"You wanna come in and see?"

Big and Little John were in the back seat. Big John looked at the baby, and the baby shrugged. "Sure," said Big John for the both of them.

The huge Lakota had gone through an amazing change in the past weeks. He was still huge, still covered with scars and crude tattoos, yet Claire noticed an undeniable serenity as well. He unbuckled the baby, palmed him in one huge hand, and followed Claire toward the front of the radio station.

Workers from the sign company were switching out the Plexiglas marquee. The new sign read, "KCAH-AM 1620, the Voice of Truth." Stan was given carte blanche on design, and since he had no skills or flair in that line, he decided on simple pica font, like you'd find on old manual typewriters. Claire decided she liked it. Simple, no frills, just hard journalism. *Go get 'em, buddy.*

Walking through the open door, she realized she was going in the back entry instead of the front. The whole radio station ran along the lower floor of an office building, and most of the rooms had windows that looked out over the back parking lot. All the doors were propped open, and through the windows, she could see that a final cleanup was underway. Four people with shop vacs, carpet vacuums, dustpans, and brooms were attacking the final layers of drywall dust with gusto.

She walked in and saw the bottom half of a large, lumpish form working on some wiring under a console. She recognized it as belonging to Matt Bradley, the kid who'd moved over from Hall Media, a tireless and morose worker.

"Hey, Matt." She kicked his shoes to get his attention.

He scooted back a bit and looked up at her through grimy glasses. "Hey, Claire." He sounded glum.

"You know where Stan is?"

Matt heaved a heavy sigh. "Probably up front." He pointed with a screwdriver and then scooted back under.

Cal and Wes, her cousins, were running some tests on the studio—Wes with an oscilloscope, Cal checking the levels on the phone as it ran through the board.

"Stan here?" Claire asked.

Both nodded, and Wes said, "Yep."

Cal nodded to both Johns. "Hey."

"Looks nice." And she meant it. It was nothing fancy but had lots of natural light and what looked like pretty good equipment.

"Walls are weird." Wes nodded to the corners.

Whoever designed the building had decided that the whole structure would be built at odd angles. Each room was a parallelogram with a forty-degree corner and a one-hundred-degree corner. Standard square cabinets and equipment looked awkward. Claire saw their point and shrugged.

Stan walked in with that intense look he had, saw her and the two Johns, and his face broke into a smile. "Hey."

She smiled back. "Hey yourself." Then with a gesture, she said, "Looks pretty good."

"It's getting there." He waved his hand around the room. "Signal is up and solid. We're looping Frank Sinatra's 'The Best Is Yet to Come.' Monday at six a.m., we'll have our first newscast and break the format. One of the production rooms is ready. The other might take till next week. Matt Bradley—you met him?"

Claire nodded.

"He's got the networks we need dialed in on the satellite. CBS Radio is available, so we're using that as our primary. I'm meeting with the staff in an hour to go over assignments and shifts."

Claire watched him while he talked, the energy pulsing off of him in waves. He had a natural command and authority, and it was a joy to watch. Claire had met the owner once and dismissed him for what he was. Charlie Hofer was a weasel and a snake, and his motives were shady, but he'd hired Stan, and he'd started something. Claire had a feeling Hofer would get a little more than he'd bargained for.

"So you met everybody, then?" The way Stan said it made her give him a look.

"Pretty sure."

"You met Doris?"

"Who?"

Stan paused. "Yeah… kind of a surprise. She got fired from her old job, and the circumstances were such that…"

Cal and Wes had stopped working and were watching the conversation with quiet amusement. "She came through the back way," offered Cal, probably the longest sentence he'd used in the last year.

Stan cleared his throat. "You probably know about her. It's Charlie's ex-wife."

"Veronica?" Claire's eyebrows shot up.

"Her real name is Doris."

"Ex-wife?"

"Yeah." Stan colored a little bit. "Charlie dropped the divorce papers on her while we were meeting, and he tossed her out." He added lamely, "It was a brutal thing to see, and I just couldn't…"

"You hired a *stripper* for a receptionist?"

Stan was talking faster. "She *was* a stripper, but she did a surprising amount of bookwork for Charlie and is familiar with a lot of the software, so I thought that maybe…"

Claire stepped closer to Stan, leveling him a hard look. "Listen, buddy boy…"

What she was going to say was interrupted by the woman herself stepping into the doorway. "Hey, Stan, I was looking over the office supplies, and I…" She stopped in midsentence, surprised, catching sight of the semicircle facing her—Stan, Cal, Wes, Claire, and the two Johns.

Claire looked at her hard. Doris was almost six feet tall with blond hair piled on her head. She had a cautious, almost frightened look in her eyes and an enormous chest draped over with a conservative blouse and cardigan sweater.

She looked at Claire and took a half step back. She held her chin up a trifle, knowing that she was being judged, eyes bright with the sting of shame.

Two seconds went by in an eternity.

Then Little John thrust himself forward with his arms out. Big John stepped forward and held the baby out in a massive hand. "Do you wanna hold him?"

Chapter 33 - Trent Wheeler

Trent Wheeler was relearning an age-old fact—shit ran downhill. The carpet had been deep, and the looks had been chilly across the table. He didn't figure it out at first. He'd never been invited to Dr. Hall's office and was looking around too much to catch the vibe. There was a plate of scones and a carafe of juice on a sideboard and coffee in one of those pots with the little candle underneath. *Swanky.*

"Would you care for something, Trent?"

He hardly noticed the touch of sarcasm in the offer. Trent started sensing he might have made a misstep when he was invited to sit. At the other end of the table. The only one with food or drink. He started to get the feeling it was some kind of test.

And I took two scones. Trent stuffed one of the scones into his mouth, trying to get rid of the evidence.

"Hungry, Trent?" There was a note of malice in the way it was phrased.

"I didn' get brefas," Trent said around his food.

The trio facing him was at the other end of a tree's worth of mahogany. Even though the table was level, Trent distinctly felt like he was looking uphill.

Dr. Hall was seated on the left, ever tan, examining his perfect nails, saying nothing, hearing everything. Technically, the two had met before. Dr. Hall was a fixture at the company Christmas party, an intimate gathering of two hundred Hall Media employees and their spouses with the radio staff relegated to the back of the room, farthest away from the stage and closer to the bar—a situation everyone was comfortable with.

The other guy was the company lawyer. He sat in the middle and was looking at the paperwork for the radio sale. Good old Diane VanDenBosch was sitting next to them. Her name was on the contract, too, but it was easy to see that she was on the other side of the table, and only one name on the contract was going to be examined. His.

"Tell me about this person, Emilio Gonzales." The lawyer was talking casually, his smooth, rich voice hiding claws.

Trent was trying to work a piece of scone out from the side of his gums without using his finger and was caught a little off guard. He was trying to remember the lawyer's name. *Minor? Meyer?*

"You mean the Mexican guy? The evangelist?"

The lawyer smiled flatly.

"Yeah, so anyway, I get a phone call, and he lookin' for a station to buy in the market, something to reach the immigrants, y'know, the ones that work at Morrell's, farm laborers."

"And how was he going to pay for this?"

"With a check, I guess." Wheeler's humor came off flat. "Uh, he said there was a bunch of stations carrying the same programs outa 'May-hee-ko.'" He used finger quotes around the Spanish pronunciation.

"What I know for sure is, the check was for two hundred thou, and not in pesos either." He looked to Diane for backing. There was none.

"And you checked into his story?"

"Story? What story?" Trent was suddenly finding it hard to swallow.

The lawyer—*Meyer! That's his name!*—pushed a picture across the table. It was a snapshot of a radio station sign that said KCAH-AM 1620, the Voice of Truth.

"Maybe that's the truth, like the Gospel truth?" Wheeler's voice lacked confidence.

"They started broadcasting this morning. KCAH is saying they are a news and information station featuring investigative journalism in the Sioux empire."

"What?"

Meyer pressed on. "The morning news anchor introduced himself as Stan Martin."

"Stan Martin?" Wheeler said, stalling. The name was familiar, but he was having a hard time thinking.

Meyer continued. "Closer scrutiny finds that this Emilio Gonzales person has not been seen in the area for months and that the purchase price and, in fact, the license of operation belong to the majority owner, Charlie Hofer."

"Charlie Hofer?" Now Wheeler was really at a loss. "You mean *the* Charlie Hofer? The sleaze king of South Dakota has purchased a news station?" He stared at the trio and got nothing but glares.

Wheeler tried bluster. "So… a crummy eight-hundred-watt AM station that barely reaches the outskirts of town is going to investigate Sioux Falls businesses? What the heck do they expect to find?"

Dr. Hall looked up at him with pure venom—or maybe it was fear.

Chapter 34 - Matt Bradley

Matt Bradley looked around the room before the morning assignments. It was seven thirty. Stan Martin was up at the white board, scribbling names underneath columns.

"Dwight. Scale of one to ten. News out of the city council meeting last night?"

Dwight was a nail chewer and was worrying a little piece of skin by the nail of his ring finger. He examined it without looking up. "Three."

Stan sighed. "Figures. Three versions. Forty-five seconds for each." He moved over to the business column. "Gretchen? Jim?"

Jim Fletcher cleared his throat, a nervous habit. He was a longtime ag reporter hired out of WNAX. He'd been second banana down there and was never going to be first, so he took the high salary Stan was offering and jumped. Thin, nervous, and suspicious, he glanced at Gretchen and jumped in. "Planting numbers are in for the state, a little higher than last year."

Stan nodded. "Jim, I'll be honest—our signal barely reaches the edge of town. We know the state runs on agriculture, but I have never seen a story on what that means exactly. Do a story on the annual impact, in dollars, per person in Sioux Falls. Make it two minutes with two versions. Gretchen?"

Gretchen Wallace was a recycled morning jock from Sioux City. She had a deep, throaty voice that was sexy and sultry and in no way matched her appearance. Her career had ended when a drunk at a bar remote asked what happened to her face. With no warning, she hauled off and kicked him square in the jewels, dropping him like a sack of wet cement. The rumor was she dropped her microphone and walked right out of the bar, both hands raised high, middle fingers offered to the bar owner and astonished patrons. She never even picked up her last check.

She got a job at Citibank in customer service, met a guy in the next cubicle, married him, and had been working for the Man for about five years. Bradley had no idea how or why she applied to work at KCAH and decided it was none of his business.

"Hank's is closing." She tossed it off the cuff and got a few looks. Hank's was a local downtown diner specializing in poor food and flagrant abuse of the state no-smoking laws. The term *smoke-filled room* described not only the behind-the-scenes deals that were made there but also the choking ambience.

Stan perked up. "Source?"

Gretchen shrugged. "Hank himself. My cousin is a nurse and was there when the doctor laid down the law to Hank—he's had two heart attacks, and this one scared the shit out of him. He told the doc he's calling a commercial real estate agent today."

"Nail it down and get it out—now. That is the top story. Get a sound bite from Hank, and I will buy you lunch."

Gretchen gave a one-sided smile and held up a cassette tape. "Right here and the noon buffet at Minerva's if you don't mind."

Stan smiled and raised an eyebrow. "Iconic Sioux Falls Establishment Calls It Quits."

He went over to another scoreboard, where the names Dwight, Gretchen, Jim, and Matt were written. At one week in, Gretchen had two hash marks, Dwight and Jim had one, and Matt had none. He grimaced. *Not for long.*

Stan put another hash mark underneath Gretchen's name. "You win this morning, Gretchen. Remember…" He looked around the room.

His gaze was intense, and Matt could feel its energy. He knew it was corny, but it reminded him of those old war movies where the commanding general gave out the mission and talked about how important victory was.

Stan repeated this same line almost word for word every day. "We are only eight hundred watts of static, but by the time we are done, we will change this city for the better, and we will not be forgotten for it."

He strode out of the room, and Matt felt the ridiculous urge to stand up. After he left, Matt flipped his pen and caught it with the same hand, staring off into space, wondering how he could land the story he knew was out there.

Chapter 35- -Lester LaFave

Lester had a system for success that had served him well. The first thing was appearance. Even when he had no money, Lester made sure he looked good. Out of prison and with no money, he found a thrift store and, in it, a complete military dress uniform that fit him beautifully. He had no idea of the rank, but it looked good. He rummaged around and found stuff to match—fatigues, camo, even dress shoes and combat boots. Hell, the uniform even had ribbons on it along with the name tag LaFave.

He tried it all on in front of a mirror, posing, constructing the life that matched the clothes. "Lester LaFave," he whispered. The name had a nice ring too.

He strode out of the store and down the street to a barbershop, head erect and hair shaggy. "Gentlemen." He folded his jacket carefully over the back of the chair and sat down.

The barber stepped right up. "High and tight?"

Lester nodded, having no idea what the barber meant. Fifteen minutes later, he looked in the mirror. His head was shaved up the sides and short and flat on top. *Nice.*

The barber took off the apron with a flourish. "On the house. *Semper Fi*."

The man who now saw himself as LaFave repeated, "*Semper Fi*."

Then he strode out the door and into the rest of his new life. It took careful listening at the local VFW to pick up details of his new life. He learned that he was a master sergeant in the Marines. He learned where he'd been stationed, what the various patches meant, and what his backstory was. He'd seen combat, of course. That meant a trip to the surplus store to pick up the needed ribbons to add to his dress uniform and to flesh out some of the other uniform stuff.

Now that his appearance was set, he worked on his second gift: lying. Lester LaFave was a master liar. He could spin a résumé out of thin air and demand compensation based on skills and experience he did not have. He was caught pretty quickly, though. A contractor, ex-marine, hired him based on his service then found out he knew absolutely nothing. Angry, the contractor dressed him down in front of everybody at a jobsite. "You don't know shit from shinola! You don't know how to plumb, wire, excavate, frame, or read a plan! Get the hell off this site, and never come back!"

Red-faced, LaFave walked to a bus station and, with eyes closed, poked his finger at a map. Sioux Falls, South Dakota, a dot on that map that seemed remote enough for his needs and big enough for his new plan of marrying his two gifts of appearance and lying with his third gift, crime.

LaFave had figured out the solution. No one was interested in résumés when something illegal or unsavory was needed. And the fees could be quite a bit higher. Off the bus, LaFave got a nice set of duds and, impeccably dressed, got some cards printed— heavy ivory stock with just his name and number. He drank soda water at the finest bars in town and introduced himself to select groups. When asked what he did, he would give a secret smile and an evasive answer.

"I... consult in private matters," he would say with a direct look that would shut down any further inquiry.

It took a few weeks before he got his first nibble. A guy named Howard, with a false laugh and a nervous look, steered a conversation toward his problem. "So my wife and I are heading out of town for the weekend... I finally got her to leave her poodle at home. The son of a bitch never did like me—growls, snaps at me. Now it's sixteen years old and has a tumor. Vet is suggesting a trip to Iowa City for emergency surgery and maybe a hip replacement. Four grand! I said we could drive down and check the place out..." He trailed off.

LaFave got the cue. "Do you want someone to take care of the dog while you're gone?"

The guy looked nervous but said nothing. LaFave got an address and some details, setting the hook. Then in an offhand way, he sipped from his drink before setting it down. "One thousand dollars."

The guy looked relieved. *Should have asked for more.*

"Do you have the money with you?" LaFave asked, and the guy nodded, looking left and right like he was in a mob movie.

LaFave, who had seen the same movie, knew what role to play. "Geez, Howard, lighten up. My coat is in the entryway, black cashmere, says LaFave on the inside breast pocket. Put the money in there, and have a nice weekend."

Killing a sixteen-year-old arthritic dog was easy. LaFave used the blanket the dog slept on to suffocate it, easy peasy. Howard was impressed and must have had a circle of friends with similar needs. LaFave did not keep count, but a few times each month, he took care of a pet while the family was gone. It was pretty easy money and a chance for his reputation to grow.

People asked about his backstory. "You special forces?"

LaFave would bark a flat laugh. "Not a chance, and if I were you, I'd leave it at that."

The capper came when a paunchy guy with a fake tan, a face-lift, and a thousand-dollar suit sat next to him at the Black Watch, a bar LaFave liked because it was dimly lit and had a guy that played pretty decent piano.

"Mr. LaFave?" The voice tried to be confident, but the mannerisms were nervous—tongue flicking at his lips, fingers fiddling with two rings or swirling the cubes around his drink.

LaFave eyed the rocks in each ring, trying to guess what his fee for Fido should be. He shrugged. "Yeah," he said as if he might as well admit it.

"You, uh, help people out, I hear. People with problems."

LaFave had seen this movie, too, and knew his line. "Depends on the problem. Depends on the fee."

"The fee is substantial." The guy darted his eyes around the room. LaFave watched him through the mirror behind the bar, waiting for him to get to the point. He was no expert, but it looked like the guy had had some work done, a face-lift probably.

LaFave had seen De Niro do a look in a movie that he liked, so he tried it out. Half-lidded, flat and cold, he paused, staring at Mr. Nervous. Then he picked up his tumbler and took a sip, the service ring on his pinky evident. "You got a problem I need to solve?" he said gently, the words wrapped in velvet.

Nervous and trying desperately not to be, the guy tried matching LaFave's manner, taking a small sip of his drink, keeping his voice equally soft. "It's my wife."

LaFave felt his heart leap in his chest. *At last! The big time.*

Chapter 36 - Matt Bradley

Matt Bradley knocked on Stan Martin's office door. The office still smelled like latex paint and drywall, like the rest of the radio station. Stan was sitting behind his desk, a big, battered relic from a place in town that sold used office equipment.

Stan's wife—an impossibly beautiful woman who intimidated the hell out of Matt—and a huge Indian dude who scared him even more had shown up one day with a load of office furniture, file cabinets, and even an old discarded phone system scavenged from the police department. With the help of the two cowboys, Cal and Wes, they'd distributed the works throughout the building, jocks laying dibs on what they wanted, shoving the mismatched styles of three decades of office decor against new tan walls. The overall impression was well worn, no-nonsense, and utilitarian.

Stan was wearing his daily uniform, a white button-down oxford shirt and rumpled khakis. A black knit tie hung like a noose on a hook in the wall, a sign that Stan was going to be at the station awhile.

"What?" Stan looked up, focused and alert.

Matt leaned into the doorframe and adjusted his glasses. "I've got an idea."

Stan looked at him, waiting.

"For a story."

Stan raised his eyebrows.

Matt sighed like the weight of the world was on his shoulders. "I've been doing a little research. About the hospital."

Stan adjusted the phone on his mostly empty desk, still waiting. Matt had learned that one of the tricks of interviewing was silence—it made people uncomfortable, got them talking more. Stan had the same habit with his employees.

Matt sighed again. He stood taller, tucked a shirttail in, adjusted his pants and glasses again, and leaned back into the doorframe. Focusing on a point on the wall behind Stan, he recited his findings.

"The medical industry is one of the largest in this country, a hundred and ninety billion dollars and growing at an annual rate of ten percent a year, making it possibly the fastest growing as well. It is also the third most common reason for death. About fifty-eight thousand malpractice lawsuits ended in payouts in the country last year on some pretty shady stuff, from Medicare fraud to unnecessary surgeries to incompetent doctors to corrupt nurses."

Stan nodded. "Sounds about right."

Matt continued. "South Dakota is small potatoes, just one fourth of one percent of the US population. So if the math works out, there should have been one hundred forty malpractice suits in South Dakota that ended with payouts."

Stan leaned forward. "And how many were there?"

"Three. Two in Rapid City and one in Aberdeen."

"None in Sioux Falls?"

"Nope."

"Maybe they're really good here." Stan gave a sardonic smile.

Matt relaxed into the doorframe. Stan was interested.

Stan leaned back into his chair, an old wooden swivel rocker that reminded Matt of the TV show *Gunsmoke*. "It would be silly to think that Hall Media would overlook any medical inconsistencies at Hall Clinic." Stan's tone was ironic. After a moment, he started ticking things off on his fingers. "One—saying that there is no story is no story. Two—wading through stacks and stacks of files, looking for irregularities, would take forever, if they even give permission, which they won't. Three—the only hope of finding a story is to find a whistleblower. Four—a whistleblower is scared for a lot of really good reasons and must be lured out slowly. Five…" Stan swiveled his chair, placed his hands on his desk and lowered his voice. "You are from this town. You know more people than you think. You are the person who will find this person, find the story, write the story and report the story."

Matt felt the hair rise on the back of his neck. *Holy shit.* Stan leveled his gaze, an icy-blue stare that made Matt's stomach flutter.

"I will tell everyone you are reporting on the economic growth of Sioux Falls as a historic piece for our weekend-programming block that will require time for you to research. Report only to me when you get something, and keep your mouth shut. This could be a little dangerous."

Chapter 37 - Trent Wheeler

Trent Wheeler had a bit of a dilemma. The Fourth of July landed on a Friday, a great chance to move his golf game to Thursday afternoon and get a jump on the weekend, but there was a big powwow scheduled at Hall Media, Thursday at one in the afternoon—big enough that they were having it on the third floor and they'd put notes everywhere. No big deal—he would claim an emergency client get-together. But at the last second, a pang of professionalism made him decide to go to the meeting. He could fake an emergency call and skip out early if it was what he suspected—a dog-and-pony show about the first two quarters' sales numbers.

It was a big deal all right. Janitors had cleared out the central reception area. A couple of big dry-erase boards were rolled up front. Tables and chairs were set up classroom style in three concentric semicircles. The first tier of chairs was dominated by the TV journalists, with a few stubborn beat reporters from the paper dug in, refusing to relinquish status to the boob tubers. The second tier was filled in with the rest of the paper staff, and the last row held curious

miscellaneous staffers and radio jocks. Trent sat
amongst them next to the table of coffee and donuts.

Up front, facing the employees, the big dogs were
perched on classy leather barstools. Dr. Harrison Hall
IV was separated off to the left, mostly observing.
Meyer the lawyer was center stage, looking
impervious and smug, probably calculating his fee by
the minute. And next to the dry-erase boards stood old
Julian Virgil Smith himself.

Julian Smith lobbied hard for Hall Media and
Hall-Hauptman Hospital and had the tan to prove it.
Lobbying in Florida with senators, lobbying with
congressional reps in Palm Beach, golf junkets, trips,
fact-finding tours—the poor guy hardly spent a day in
Sioux Falls. He had the unctuous voice of an old-time
radio announcer with the tenacious bite of a junkyard
Rottweiler.

He was now stabbing at the list of stories on the
dry-erase board with particular venom. "For eighty
years, Hall Media has been the hallmark of news
excellence. We have taken our position seriously, for
as Sioux Falls prospers, so does South Dakota, and as
South Dakota prospers, so do we. Our purpose has
been, and still is, to report news, root out corruption,
and promote our city as a great place to live and work.
So how is this…" Words failed him for a moment.
"Man"—he pointed to a picture of Charlie Hofer,
posted on the first board—"able to buy, staff,
promote, and operate an eight-hundred-watt AM
station that he bought from *us*…" Wheeler stopped
chewing his donut and slumped a little lower in his
chair. "That is now the talk of the town in just three
months?"

There was an icy pause. The only sound was the
quiet thrum of air-conditioning. No one was sure
whether it was a rhetorical question or he wanted an
answer.

One of the dry-erase boards held a list of recent stories that had been broken by KCAH. Smith slapped them with his stick one by one, like he was swatting flies. "Bitter rivalry between the city street and water departments cause wasteful delays and redundant street repair—estimated cost fifty-five million." *Slap.* "Superintendent of water department resigns after twenty years." *Slap.* "Health department accused of bribery." *Slap.* "Health department head let go." *Slap.* "Sexual harassment charges at sheriff's department— dispatchers seek damages." *Slap.* "Local plant defies EPA regulations, illegally dumps sewage." *Slap.* "Hall media flouts FCC rules regulating bandwidth."

Slap, slap, slap!

"Ladies and gentlemen, you are getting your asses handed to you by a sleazy strip-club operator who hired an alcoholic has-been and his seedy little minions, and they're operating out of a strip mall!"

Smith's outrage was like a palpable wave of heat wilting the front row of Hall Media faithful. Trent's mouth was dry around the donut. He was glad he was downrange from the fallout and secretly gleeful that the stuffed shirts were getting the full blast.

"Now, listen to this." Smith's voice grew low and venomous, biting off each syllable. "This piece of human excrement will now learn just what it means to flout the power of the real press. You will do your due diligence. You will seek and find and research and prove that only a fool starts a war with someone who buys ink by the barrel and electricity by the megawatt. You." He pointed to Meyer. "Check all the permits that allow this parasite to exist. You." He pointed to Christiansen from the crime desk. "Background checks on everybody that works there. Find dirt. Publish dirt. You." He pointed to the rest of the gathered crowd. "Get off your dead-pampered overpaid asses, and do what apparently you have been unable to do, unwilling to do, or too damn stupid to do—find news and report it!"

Trent was already sneaking out the back, grabbing an extra donut, when he heard the sentence that ruined his day.

"And for God's sake, find the stupid idiot that sold one of our stations to that weasel, fire his ass, and get the story of his firing on the air before Stan Martin does!"

Chapter 38 - Everett Meyer

Everett Meyer stood outside the room at Hall Media just after Julian Smith's tirade, waiting for the crowd to scatter. As ranking attorney for Hall, Meyer had known Smith for years and knew just how blistering his meetings could be. Even so, the latest tirade caused him to consider some of his own strategies going forward. Not necessarily an exit, but certainly a scapegoat might be needed.

"Well?" Jessica Wright, the junior attorney, walked up to him.

Meyer raised a hand, waiting for the hallway to empty. "Here." He handed her the legal pad with his notes. "You heard Smith. Head down to the records office at City Hall and check the permits on KCAH. Then check the county, the state, the FCC, you name it. I'm looking for a reason to shut them down even temporarily. This could be as minor as building-code violations or faulty tower-light inspections. Report to me at the end of each day with what you find."

Jessica took the legal pad and added it to the folder she was carrying. She didn't move.

"What?"

She shifted a bit, nodding to an empty side room. They moved inside, and he closed the door. "What is it?" he asked.

She paused as if searching for the right words. She finally said, "You heard what Julian said about the radio station. Despite their ownership, they seem to know what they're doing. I think that maybe Hall-Hauptmann is... vulnerable."

Meyer waited for her to continue.

With a nervous burst, the young attorney added, "I mean, this is ethical stuff they covered in law school. If we know of a crime, when does attorney-client privilege end? We still don't know where the Panco sales rep, Devon LaCroix, is. That seems awfully coincidental... I mean, I want to represent our clients, for sure, but I don't want to get disbarred either."

Meyer gave a rolling, unctuous laugh. "My dear, that risk, be it ever so slight, is my purview and my responsibility. Trust me, I know where the edges are, and we are far away from any kind of danger or ethical issue."

The girl sighed, and her shoulders relaxed. "Thanks, Everett. That makes me feel a lot better."

"Nothing to worry about, Jessica." He would have patted her on the shoulder—or maybe elsewhere—but you had to be careful about that stuff these days.

He watched her walk away. After she was out of sight, he came to a decision and smiled. He'd found his scapegoat.

Chapter 39 - Jessica Wright

After the meeting run by Julian Smith, the Hall Hospital lobbyist, Jessica Wright, had been worried about what her possible role might be in some shady business. Then she talked to Everett Meyer and felt a little better. Then she had a conversation with her college ethics professor and felt worse.

Then after stewing about it for a day or two, she remembered some of the stuff her grandpa Wright would say: "I may have been born at night, but I wasn't born last night."

A feisty rancher, the elder Wright did a lot of deals on a handshake, but he'd told Jessica many times, "Rosie! I may settle on a handshake, but I never shake a hand until I know the person it's attached to."

Then she remembered the look Everett Meyer had given her and finally made up her mind. The South Dakota bar was located in Pierre, the capital. Jessica took the weekend to visit her family and the day off on Monday to meet with an advisory member of the bar. As she waited for the appointment, she patted the file that held notes and recordings taken around the

events surrounding the botched surgery on Martha
Elaine Sanderson by Dr. Harrison Benjamin Hall V.

She thought about Everett Meyer and smiled
grimly. *Sorry, pal.*

Chapter 40 - Harrison Hall

The good doctor Harrison Benjamin Hall IV was at his home on the Oaks, staring down the sun-dappled summer fairway and a thousand yards beyond that, trying to see all the moves, countermoves, deceits, and deceptions that would get rid of his problem and leave him in the clear.

He should just let his spoiled brat of a son face the music, but of course, he had the same name, and even a little bit of splatter back on the famous Hall name he himself had worked so hard to burnish and maintain was unacceptable.

Deidre was even worse. He did not fully know—did not want to know—but he was certain that she was behind the disappearance of that Devon LaCroix salesman.

"Bitch." He allowed himself to whisper the word in the privacy of his plush office. She'd found a way to exploit his weakness, he had to admit, but now he had the situation in hand, and just like cutting out a malignant tumor, he was ready to be rid of the problem forever. The man in the bar, LaFave, was unsavory, certainly, but willing and competent. He'd looked at a calendar. Hall planned to make a trip to the Florida Keys to spend a week or so at the condo. That would give him an excellent alibi.

There was a discreet knock on the door. "Dr. Hall? Mr. Warner is here. Do you have time?"

Hall smiled grimly. He knew what this was probably about. "Yes, see him in… Scotch, Chet?"

Chet Warner steamed in and was swearing before the door was closed behind him. "Did you hear the news this morning?"

Hall feigned innocence. "News?"

"That rat bastard Charlie Hofer and his muckraking piece-of-shit radio station! I'll sue!"

Hall handed Chet a tumbler and told him to calm down, needling him with "Not the language of a gentleman, Chet."

"It's the government! It's how it's done! Everybody does it! You want to get a chance at a bid, you have to talk to the right people, and to talk to the right people, you have to donate funds."

"Five hundred thousand dollars is a big donation."

Warner stiffened. "So you did hear about it."

Hall shrugged. "I thought it was a rumor." In truth, Hall had listened to the whole story on the 7:05 morning news, the radio station signal so weak he had to plug it in by the window and sort through the static.

Warner Manufacturing had gotten a government contract to manufacture storage tanks for the defense department, a multimillion-dollar deal that was five years old. That was far enough back to make Chet Warner forget how much his mistress—a leggy college grad promoted out of her junior year into private-executive-secretary status—remembered.

The secretary had become spoiled by her instant success and entitlement and access to much information. When Chet got bored with her and cut her loose, she'd gotten even with him and was undoubtedly the "unnamed source" mentioned on the air. That had been gossip around the country club, and it was usually accurate, but hearing the dirty laundry broadcast for all of Sioux Falls to hear as confirmed fact was secretly delicious.

"Sophie will have my nuts!"

Hall could imagine. Sophie was no one to trifle with. Her brother was a lawyer in Omaha and would know how to extract the most cash in a divorce.

"How can I help, old man?" Hall occasionally used British slang at the club. He felt it suited his status.

"Harrison, my good friend." Warner had never used the term *friend* before with Hall. He was leaning in for leverage. "You have to stop this guy. You have connections in the media. You can't let this little prick run down pillars of the community like this!"

Hall clucked his tongue, sipped his Scotch, and thought about his secret weapon, Lester LaFave.

Chapter 41 - Lester LaFave

Lester LaFave loved Sioux Falls. He stretched out alongside the luscious naked body of Deidre Hall, congratulating himself on his good fortune. Hall had given him a name and a picture and an address. The picture had piqued his interest, the address even more so.

A big believer in the direct approach, LaFave tried a Robert Mitchum line out at the front door, walking past the maid.

"Mrs. Hall? The name's LaFave. Can I come in?"

The tall ice queen with nails like fangs and a formfitting designer housedress stared at him disdainfully. "No. Get out."

"Not so fast, doll."

"Did you call me *doll?*"

LaFave backpedaled. "Listen, this is a matter of a person's life." He looked meaningfully at the too-near maid.

So that got him in the door, into the living room. Then it got him a top-shelf Beefeaters over ice, and that got him her whole story, the iced facade crumbling, the tears leaking down and ruining her mascara, the choking sobs. And that led to an awkward hug, a feverish kiss, a ripped shirt and dress, and finally, a whispered confession. "This is the first time I've ever felt safe."

LaFave traced a finger up and down the back of the sleeping wife of Dr. Benjamin Hall IV, calculating the value of what he could see around him, estimating the value of what he couldn't see, and deciding that an alliance with the widow of a doctor was far more lucrative than a one-time fee for getting rid of an unwanted spouse.

Chapter 42 - John Returns From Hunt

John sat on a stack of drywall outside the project house, drinking a cup of coffee out of a thermos, baby John perched on his lap. *Going to be a hot one today, no doubt.* The heavy, dirty work was done. The inside of the house was stripped of lathe and plaster, tons and tons of it, all hauled out in plastic barrels or dumped out of convenient windows. The windows themselves were gone, leaving empty, staring eyes out of the bones of the house. The new windows were on order. The millwork inside the house had been carefully removed, labeled, and stacked in the garage. Claire was his undisputed boss and a woman who had earned his loyalty. Brisk, no-nonsense, she was a person who told him what the general task was, the objective for the day, and then together, they set about doing it. She was better at the fine work and knew some things about construction he did not. He was better at high work and heavy work. She would show him what she was doing, teaching him without condescending, and he would help with heavier things, also without being demeaning. They were a good team, centered on a task to do and a baby to watch.

And John loved that baby. He could not explain it. There was a power to that solid little boy and a depth to those bottomless eyes that soothed the hidden wounded places inside John, places that counselors or elders had tried to reach but had failed. Both he and Claire knew about this power but did not discuss it. How to talk about what there were no words for?

Instead, they brought the baby along, working to keep him away from dusty, dangerous places during the construction, keeping him nearby. The baby John would observe with his serious, almost comical expression, making no noise, no sound, but with a deep comprehension. It was weird.

A car door slammed, and both Johns looked over. It was Doris, the woman from the radio station. She brought lunch by the work site most days.

The gossip from the station was that she was there to see him, that they had a thing going. A few braver souls had approached the big Lakota and tried to lure him in. "She's got somethin' for ya, huh?" Their attempts fell flat under John's expressionless stare. In truth, John was drawn to the tall blonde, but not merely for her physical appearance.

"Hey, John. Hey, John." She addressed them each separately. She had a sack of food. "Meatloaf sandwiches. Leftovers from supper."

She set the bag on the drywall and perched next to him. John had found out that she was a good cook and that she liked to watch a hungry man eat. But more than that, she liked to hold the baby.

"Hey, little man." She held the boy up. "Ohh, you're a little chunk, aren't you?"

The baby did not smile. He seldom did, but he did have a way of looking pleased. He gave her that pleased look and, with a chubby little hand, touched her cheek gently, looking deep into her eyes. Instantly, tears sprang up and ran down her cheeks. It had happened many times before. No one was surprised.

"Weird, huh?" John shook his head. He knew how she felt.

Doris's eyes were closed as she rocked the baby against her. The baby's eyes were closed, too, his little hand patting her softly to the rhythm of the rocking. It was soothing to watch. John Returns From Hunt found himself smiling gently.

"Some day, he will heal you all up, and there will be no more tears." John was not much of a talker, but he felt a kinship he could not explain with this wounded white woman.

"Yeah," Doris murmured, patting the baby, who patted her.

Claire appeared, coated with dust, looking on at the scene. She and Doris had an unspoken truce, maybe even a friendship, bonded by the baby. They were part of the same group, which defied a name. Not a team. Maybe a family.

"Hey." She sat next to John, fished a sandwich out of the sack, and took a bite. "Hmm. Meatloaf." Claire liked a homemade meal too. "Whaddaya hear from Stan?"

Doris, eyes still closed, murmured back, "He's doin' what he was hired to do. Stir up stuff. We're getting a lot more phone calls. Got a letter from an attorney today, threatening something."

"What for?"

"Dunno. Some story that ran. Stan'll figure it out. Charlie's got enough lawyers to stop anything. No need to worry."

At that moment, Little John's eyes flew open and looked at Big John, his face somber. Big John felt a sudden tremor of fear.

Chapter 43 - Matt Bradley

Matt Bradley had family in Sioux Falls since way back. He had dozens of cousins, and hardly any of them had moved away. Friendly uncles and doting aunts, most of them blue-collar, were all connected to the pulse of the town they'd grown up in and loved.

He started with Uncle Larry, manager for a beer distributor. "Hey, Uncle Larry, where do the nurses and hospital types hang out?"

His uncle set down the sixteen-gallon keg and grinned. He hefted the sixteen gallons with ease—the joke he always made was that it was light beer. "Nurses, huh? Well, there's a bunch that hang out at the Crow Bar. They got a ladies' night on Thursdays and Fridays that packs them in. If the Pomp Room has a decent band, a lot of chickies go there. Course, it's so loud it's hard to make any time, if you know what I mean."

"What about to blow off steam—a quieter place closer to the hospital?"

"Nah. You never blow off steam next to where you work. Too many witnesses. I'd prolly try the Coachlite... out by the mall. Drinks are cheap, and they make a wicked Long Island iced tea. I think Millie's kid Tyler works there."

"Thanks, Uncle." Tyler would be Matt's cousin on his mom's side, a big kid who used to play for O'Gorman High School before he blew out a knee.

"Hey, Matt," his uncle called. Matt looked back to see his uncle winking at him. "On account of your ma would never let me hear the end of it… make sure she's Catholic."

Chapter 44 - Janet Brecht

Sean Clark, Ann Johnson, and Janet Brecht were huddled in the back booth of the Coachlite bar, hammering Long Island iced teas. Janet should have been in the bag, but the term *scared sober* was working fine for her at the moment.

"This shit is seriously scary. Where the f..." She looked around the empty bar and lowered her voice. "Where the fuck is Devon LaCroix?"

Sean Clark shrugged. He was scared, too, she could tell, but was trying not to be. "He's gone, left. Probably got a better offer somewhere else. The guy could sell ice to Eskimos." He did not sound convinced.

"I call bullshit." Ann was so scared she was wearing big Jackie O sunglasses, ridiculous in the dimly lit bar. "Devon was making bank working here. Yeah, he could've gone to Chicago, Denver, maybe Minneapolis, but there are way more reps there— more competition, tighter margins."

Janet glanced at Ann. She was pretty sure much of what Ann knew about Devon LaCroix came from post-coital cigarettes at the Holiday Inn, but she was in no mood to tease. None of them were. "You heard what that shyster Meyer said. You think it's a coincidence that Devon is gone right after that shit show with Hall Five?"

There was a moody pause while all three drank deeply. Sean spoke first. "You heard about that new radio station, the Voice of Truth?"

"Hell no." Ann was shaking her head vigorously. "No damn way." She unconsciously flipped the collar on her coat. With the sunglasses, she now looked like freaking Mata Hari.

Chad pressed forward. "Listen, I don't want to be a whistleblower either. We don't have to say a name—we can be anonymous. I just think it's a little dangerous to be three nobodies when there used to be four."

Ann's hand was shaking. "Shit, Chad! You think they did something to Devon."

"No, I didn't say that. I just think the Hall family would pay a lot of money to a lot of people to keep this whole thing quiet. Including a cocky sales rep."

Janet was toying with her drink and thinking about her Visa bill and mortgage, measuring her fear against her debt. Sean was right. This story could mean a lot.

Chapter 45 - Matt Bradley

Matt was built for the grind of investigative work. Relentless and plodding, he was convinced that he had an idea about a story coming out of the Hall-Hauptman Hospital and was equally convinced that none of his ways to crack the story were any good. But he kept at it, adding all the little bits of ideas to his daily work, like when he'd added a customer to his paper route when he was a kid. Just one more thing to follow up on, one more place to check, one more person to keep an eye on.

Tyler was his cousin and, like all the Bradleys, was built on the large side. He had a slight limp but handled all the work of the bar with leisurely ease. The Coachlite was not high on anyone's list of popular hangouts, but it had its clientele, a quiet group of heavy drinkers who sat in the cave-dark bar like depressed insomniacs.

"Hey, Ty." Matt plopped onto the bar stool nearest the door, waiting for his eyes to adjust to the dark.

"Hey." Tyler drew a draft and slid it down the bar. It looked like a juice glass in Matt's hand.

"You got anything?"

Tyler shrugged like he didn't get it. "Got any what?"

Matt sighed with patience. "I don't exactly know. Uncle Larry said a lot of nurses, doctors hang out here."

Tyler barked a short laugh. "Doctors? Hell no. Nurses..." He nodded to a trio down the way, huddled in a corner. "There's a few that come in."

Matt drained the glass in a quick swallow. "So here's the deal. I think there may be... something shady going on at the hospital, and like I said before, I don't even know what it is." Tyler rolled his eyes as Matt went on. "So if I worked at the hospital, and if I was involved with something shady, I'd probably talk about it with my buddies somewhere private." He motioned with his hand. "Like this place."

Tyler looked blank.

Matt stood up and tossed a bill on the counter. "Look, if you see anything that looks weird involving nurses and such"—he nodded to the three sitting around a small forest of empty Long Island iced tea glasses—"like, say, those three down there, doing or saying something or acting... I dunno, weird, lemme know."

Tyler shrugged. "That's it?"

"Yep."

Tyler took the bill and made change. Matt fished out the bills and left the coins.

"You really think anything is gonna happen here?"

Matt sighed and got ready to head out to his next stop. "Nope."

Chapter 46 - Don Keshane

It was tough sledding, no doubt about it. Don worked his old list of radio clients, and the banks said no. All of them. Many had loans with Hall-Hauptman Hospital and did not want to endanger that in any way. Same with construction firms. Same with big retail and grocery. It seemed no matter who he talked to, they were either friends with or wanted to be friendlier with the biggest employer in town and did not want to create trouble with the biggest media partner in town.

Don tapped the steering wheel of the Caddy, thinking. *If I can't find their friends, who are their enemies?*

He found some sympathy with Dr. Winston Williams, a smooth and manicured chiropractor who touted various oils and therapies that were "well beyond the understanding of those Neanderthals at Hall." Don sold him an annual package of morning news, setting the rate fifteen percent higher and then cutting a deal that made the doc happy and still got Don his thirty percent.

Up and down the street he went, wheeling and dealing. In many ways, it was tougher than other jobs he'd had—all he had to sell was a crummy AM signal that barely left town. But on the other hand, it was easier too. Donnie no longer had to know about all the other stations, formats, rate cards, and programming. All he had was a piece of cardboard with the rates on it and his persuasive patter, selling all who would listen on the importance of a free press and David and Goliath and the Voice of Truth.

Arnie and June Booth were the last call of the day and the biggest. The legal duo specialized in representing the little guy and had done pretty well at it. They were the biggest name in the eastern half of South Dakota. A person would have to go to Denver or maybe Omaha to find a bigger name. Booth and Booth specialized in malpractice and OSHA violations. Arnie was the legal mind, handling the case law and research, impeccably dressed with cufflinks and two-tone wingtips. He was somewhat of a dandy. June was the face of the company, a high-wattage force of nature. Her unflappable wit, dry delivery, and roguish sense of fun made her a hit with juries while never crossing too far over a line with the judges. She was like a teacher's pet who knew when to stop pushing.

June Booth happened to be in when Don was dropping off a proposal for Arnie.

"Oho! The Voice of Truth! So you're the little thorn in the side of Hall Media, huh?"

"Saving Sioux Falls from media mediocrity!" Don was wearing a charcoal suit and silk tie, not quite to Arnie's sartorial splendor, but he had a fresh carnation in the lapel, and he could see that June approved.

Arnie tossed the rate card on the desk. "I can't get it where I live, and I can't hardly get it here in the office."

Don was ready for that one, nodding in agreement. "Folks all over town are hopping their cars to catch the news, buying ham radios to pick up the AM signal better. That means they are *listening.*"

Arnie was not done complaining. "I missed the interview with the guy from Warner Manufacturing—"

June cut in. "Chester 'Chet' Warner… I caught it on the drive in. You could hear the guilt dripping off every statement."

"Why don't you send me the transcript?" Arnie said. Don turned and looked at him, and Arnie continued. "Why don't you email me the article about Warner?"

Don thought fast, making things up as he went. "That's part of our soon-to-be-launched service. We'll be sending out the transcript of each story we do each day to our subscribers."

June looked interested. "How much is that?"

Don thought fast again and came up with a number double what he thought it would take.

"Sign me up." Arnie shrugged as if it was a no-brainer.

Damn it! Too low. Then Donnie said casually, "You interested in the combo rate, commercial on the station and in the email?"

June and Arnie shrugged again. "How much?"

Don took a breath and tripled the rate card, adding, "That's our introductory price for a six-month trial."

Arnie and June shrugged again. "Might as well try it."

Don Keshane drove off in his drop-top red Caddy with a check, kicking himself as a fool. He pounded the steering wheel and muttered, "Too low again."

Chapter 47 - Stan

Stan Martin stared across the desk at the newly reinvented Don Keshane and wondered if he had created a monster. Donnie was dressed in a navy-blue double-breasted blazer, cream-colored slacks, a knotted navy tie with cream polka dots, and cordovan Italian leather loafers with tassels. He adjusted the off-white carnation in his lapel and leaned leisurely back in his chair with a self-assured smile. All that was missing was the yacht.

Settling in, Stan put on his game face. *Time for round two.*

A week earlier, Donnie had come in with a huge check for a nonexistent newsletter sent out via email. He tried to slip it into the stack on Doris's desk. This was met with immediate blowback up and down the hallway that Donnie tried to bluff away. "How hard can it be to send an email a few times a day of the stories you've already written?"

Stan now had to manage it. He called over Jim Fletcher, the ag newsman. "You're the fastest typist we have and have good editing skills. How long would it take to transcribe a newscast and send it out in an email?"

Jim thought for a minute. "Maybe half an hour."

Stan nodded. "And adding and correcting email addresses... say maybe up to fifty a day?"

Jim tilted his head. "About the same, I suppose."

Stan looked at both of them. "Donnie here has sold something we don't have and I've never heard of before but might turn out to be a pretty good thing for the station. Every hour in morning drive, you convert our newscasts to an email, make sure the spelling and grammar is right, drop me a copy, and you might as well send it to Doris too. She will pay you for each newscast you send out and take it out of Don's check." He quoted a fee that made Jim smile and Don pout.

"Don't worry about it, Don. You are one heck of a salesman." To prove it, Stan fished another contract out and scanned it. "What does 'studio sponsor' mean?"

"It's genius is what it is. I've got a cousin that's in charge of promotions for a minor league baseball club in Ohio. He's got more ways to sell stuff than you can imagine. Some of them can work for us. Have you heard of the C, M, and G Railroad?"

Stan shook his head.

"Neither has anyone else. Stands for Canadian, Mississippi, and Gulf Railroad—a new rail line bringing down grain from the north and oil from the gulf, all the cities on the route getting schmoozed... promising a good deal for everyone. A lobbying firm is trying to get all the states on board—Feds, railroad commission, all that stuff."

"And...?"

"And it's too early by far to drop in ads for a railroad that doesn't exist, I mean what would you say? A bill hasn't even been introduced yet. Heck the company *logo* hasn't been vetted yet, but the news can be broadcast from the 'C, M, and G Railroad studios.' Lets the idea of a railroad seep into the minds of the population, maybe helps come lobbying time. And it doesn't count in the inventory. No clutter, free money."

"How much?" Stan asked, and Don told him. Stan shook his head with a wry smile. "All right. I'll mention it at the next staff meeting."

Chapter 48 - Lester LaFave

Lester LaFave was in his usual seat at the bar. By that point, he was somewhat of a fixture. The bartender knew him by drink and gave him the space to conduct his business, along with a certain cagey respect. LaFave nurtured this by giving the barkeep an aloof nod and a hefty tip. *That's right, asshole, I'm Lester LaFave.*

This LaFavian act had gotten a little more intricate with the arrival of Dr. Harrison Hall. LaFave gauged him carefully in the mirror over the bar as he walked in, trying to guess if Hall knew LaFave was shtupping the missus. The nervous way he sidled up to the stool next to him made him think not.

LaFave stirred the drink in front of him with a ringed pinky and took a sip. Then after a bored pause, he looked at the mirror behind the bar. "Yeah?"

Hall lifted a hand to the bartender, trying to match LaFave's cool demeanor. "I have another problem."

LaFave cocked his head and took another sip. "*Another* problem?"

Flustered, Hall spilled a little of the drink in front of him and made a little show of mopping it up with a spare napkin. "This one isn't as permanent." Hall tried to look confident. "There's a person saying some disturbing things about important people and needs to be taught a lesson."

LaFave savored the moment. "So, lemme get something straight. I'm taking care of a woman for you, and now you want me to take care of a man too?" he said, forcing Hall to spell it out.

"Shh!" The sound came out almost involuntarily. "No, I mean the first person, that's the same. That can happen next week when I'm in Florida. The second person is not a permanent answer, just you getting a message across in a..." Hall searched for a word. "Painful way. Let him know the risks of insulting the wrong people."

"This second guy got a name?"

"Yes, but I want the punishment to be more than just physical." Hall touched an envelope in his pocket. "He has a wife and a kid."

"A kid?" LaFave decided he didn't really care if it was a kid, a grandma, or a golden retriever, but knew he could probably get some leverage on the price if it seemed like it bothered him.

He drank a sip and turned slowly to face Hall. He'd heard that movies stars in a close-up looked at just one eye of the other actor. That way, their eyes wouldn't flick back and forth. He tried it, like in a movie he'd seen Robert Mitchum in, staring at Hall's right eye for the long slow count of ten.

"We better talk about this someplace else."

Chapter 49 - Matt Bradley

Matt Bradley was plodding out to his car—another day of making the rounds, looking for something that statistically should be there but could not be found. Stan hadn't said anything about the lack of progress. Rather, he'd been encouraging, saying, "It'll come. Just keep your eyes open."

Yeah, yeah, sure. Eyes open. He was preoccupied enough that he almost ran into the guy with the card outside the station.

"Uh, excuse me. I'm from out of town. I was told there was an independent radio station that handled investigative news?" Young, tan, the guy looked like a gym teacher or a golf pro.

Matt nodded glumly. "Yeah, this is it."

The golf pro looked both relieved and concerned. Matt assumed he was glad he'd finally found the place but taken aback by the actual studios.

Matt caught the vibe and felt a little defensive. "It's a radio station. Nobody cares what it looks like as long as it sounds good."

"Yeah, sure, I get it." The guy shrugged and smiled. "Back in the day, I did a little DJ work in college."

Matt sighed deeply. "Yeah." Then again with great effort, he said, "So there's application forms at the front desk…"

"No, no." Golf Pro laughed sheepishly. "No, I just am looking for… well, it's about my aunt. I've been trying to get her some help, trying to find some answers, but I keep getting the runaround. I told my Uncle Earl I'd try to help, but no matter who I talk to, it seems like I'm being stonewalled."

Matt resisted the temptation to look at his watch. This guy was holding him up, but there didn't seem any option outside of just walking away. He tried a half turn toward his car, a hint that the conversation was over.

The guy pressed on. "I'm not really the kind of person to go to the press, and I'm certain there's a good reason, but I just don't have time to keep driving back and forth from my practice…"

Practice. Matt slowly turned and looked. "Practice?"

The guy gave him his card: *William C. Sanderson, MD. Doctor of Orthopedic Surgery ABOS/AAOS/AANA*

"And you think you're getting stonewalled?"

The guy started backpedaling. "Well, medicine is not an exact science, and there are many, many reasons why a surgery would not have the optimum outcomes."

Matt was leaning over the golf-pro doctor with a predatory eagerness. "But you're a surgeon. You aren't just an ordinary person. If you have doubts or questions about a surgery, you must have some reason for it."

"Yes, I do, but I also don't want to ruin the reputation of a fine hospital through blind accusations—"

Matt was giving him the *Yeah, yeah, get to the point* motion with his hands as he cut him off. "Name the doctor. Name the hospital."

Taken aback, Dr. Sanderson opened and shut his mouth twice before saying, "Hall-Hauptman. And the doctor is named Benjamin Hall. I'm told he's related to the founder."

Matt closed his eyes and smiled. *Bingo.*

Chapter 50 - Harrison Hall IV

Doctor Benjamin Harrison Hall IV fumbled with the keys to the carriage house, running on the edge of sanity. *Shit, shit, shit, shit, SHIT!* This whole thing was one big shit show, and he felt like he was on the very edge of falling into the shit himself, pulling the entire Hall legacy down with him. It was like skiing two feet in front of an avalanche, but there wasn't much he could do about it. He pressed his forehead against the cold stone wall of the renovated carriage house that at one time held horses and carriages and tack and hay but now held two Mercedes and a Lamborghini.

Deep breaths. Willing himself to calm down, Hall focused on what he could control, forgetting about things that couldn't be undone.

At least he had Deidre taken care of. He shuddered at the cool and calm way the psychopath LaFave was ready to handle her and the reporter from KCAH. He didn't want Stan Martin killed, just shaken up a little, but the way LaFave had shrugged about beating up a woman and her toddler made Hall's blood run cold. Hopefully, he would take care of both problems quickly and leave town. A guy like that was bad for the reputation of Sioux Falls.

Hall checked the date on his watch. *Ten days, tops, then it will be over.* By then he would be well south of the snow and ice-cold weather. He shivered involuntarily. The detached carriage house was a nice idea in the summer but a pain in the ass in the winter. He plugged his key into the doorway and activated the door opener, a relic from the thirties that was mostly a nuisance. Come spring he'd have the whole thing torn down and replaced. *Piece of crap.*

"Excuse me, Dr. Hall?"

"Shit!" He jumped and wheeled.

He hadn't seen the nurse in the winter coat until she was right up on him. He frowned. He did not like low-level doctors approaching him, much less nurses, much less nurses on his property.

"What are you doing here? How did you get in here?" True, the building he called home was technically hospital property, and true, Hall-Hauptmann personnel could have access if needed, but this kind of sneaking around was unacceptable. He would see what he could do to have her fired.

The nurse stepped closer. She looked vaguely familiar in a way that set an alarm off inside his head. She was obviously a nurse. Underneath her blue down coat, he could see the blue scrubs. Her hair was pulled up, and she wore cushioned white athletic shoes and too much makeup around her eyes.

She motioned back over her shoulder. "I took the bus. I didn't want to park in front and, you know, cause a scene." She stepped forward knowingly. "My name's Janet Brecht. I was on the surgical team with your son. The one Mr. Meyer the lawyer wanted to talk to us about?"

He leaned back away from her frosty breath. "Yes?"

"Well, it's just that I've had some concerns, stuff that's been bothering me. And I want to talk to some people about it, but it doesn't seem like it would be right to talk to the police or to a reporter… I think it would be best if maybe… just you and I could talk about it. Come to an agreement."

The words came out like a well-rehearsed script—the look, the smile, the nod. Perhaps it was the fact that she seemed so certain of herself, or maybe it was his fear—or maybe her *rudeness*—that made him a little bit crazy.

"And you came here to my house?" He almost shouted the words, outraged that this… *nurse* would have the gall to approach him at his home.

Alarmed, the nurse suddenly stepped back. And slipped.

Ice and snow were a continuous part of winters in South Dakota, and most people slipped and fell at least once each winter. The rustic cobbled walk that led from the home to the carriage house collected melted snow from its gabled roof, a season-long menace. The nurse slipped on that ice patch, which was slick as a skating rink, and went down in an inglorious pratfall, both feet splaying out with tremendous force.

Reeling her hands back to catch her balance, she fell. *Kloch.* With a noise that ironically sounded like a horse shoe striking pavement, the back of her head hit squarely on the corner of the hitching post—a square pillar of purple quartzite—just above where the spinal column entered the skull base.

Open-mouthed, Hall watched her convulse on the ground, thrashing about with spasmodic jerks, eyes wide open in shock, mouth open in a soundless scream. *A complete accident.*

Hall looked up toward the house. It was empty, of course. No one was home. Trees shielded the walkway from the neighbors, and the carriage house shielded the view from the street.

No car. No, she said she took the bus. No witnesses.

The cold air was silent, with just the sound of her limbs and body thrashing, thrashing. He thought about calling an ambulance or the police or both then thought about the questions that might come up. He watched her convulsions through a series of emotions—horror, alarm, worry, fear—then finally had no emotions at all, just thought.

He checked her pulse at the neck. *Not dead.* He waited a little longer. Then she was dead. He sighed with surprising relief. For once, the worst thing that could happen did not happen. For once, luck was on his side.

He closed the door to the carriage house for privacy then went inside to get some garbage bags.

Chapter 51 - Marvin Carlson

What Marvin liked about his job at Hall-Hauptmann was the hours and the autonomy. No one bothered him as he cleaned the building, and no one told him how to do it, either. He was a vet, saw some action, and was admittedly a little screwed up after it. He did not like crowds or people or sudden movements or loud noises.

Being a nighttime janitor at the hospital was fine with him. Every night was like clockwork, same chores at the same times, steady, steady, steady. His mother had thought he was too good for the night work, thought he would get bored with it, and maybe over time, he would. But for the past eleven years, the soothing monotony had been a balm for his soul.

At 1:35 a.m., with the floors swept and scrubbed, Marvin jangled his keys as he walked to the incinerator. The hospital produced a varying amount of medical waste each day, and 1:35 to 2:45 was when Marvin would toss the bright-red biohazard bags into the hopper and hit the switch. *Woom!* There'd be a soft explosion of gas igniting and the warmth of the gas jets doing their job, consuming the waste into powdery fragments. Then he would hit the processor button, and the fragments would be evenly ground into Grape-Nuts-sized granules, then poured into a gray plastic sack and sent off to the dumpster by three in the morning, like clockwork.

So it was extremely upsetting to have his routine upset by some nervous jerk with a clipboard and some heavy boxes.

"Who're you?" Marvin was blunt. No one was supposed to bother him.

"I'm Dr. Hall."

The guy said it like it was supposed to mean something. Marvin just stared.

"Look. Didn't you hear from your supervisor when you reported in?" The intruder puffed out his cheeks in frustration. "We have boxes and boxes of documents to be shredded, and the shredder is down for service work. We decided to use the incinerator."

"Okay." It was not okay, but Marvin shrugged and waited for the guy to leave.

"It's sensitive material. I have to be the one to incinerate it. Lots of protected documents and patient files." The doctor said it in a hurry, like Marvin was the one who was breaking his routine. *Asshole.*

"I'll be done in about half an hour." He gave a shushing movement with his hands like he was trying to sweep Marvin out into the hall without touching him.

Marvin sighed. Brass was brass, military or civilian. He wasn't happy about it, but what could he do, anyway? These asshole pricks pushed people around like they were the be-all and end-all, like they knew everything and other people knew nothing.

He shuffled out into the hall, shaking his head. *Jerk.* Everyone knew to be careful about the plastic. If there was too much, it would jack around with the smoke particulates, and here this asshole was, burning up a bunch of papers—not in cardboard boxes, which would make sense, but in plastic tubs, sealed and unwieldy, looked like they weighed about sixty to eighty pounds apiece. The jerk doctor was heaving them up onto the table and shoving them into the incinerator like he was trying to set a record.

Marvin thought about helping him just as a way to get him the hell out of there faster, but he decided not to. *Jerk.*

About forty minutes later, just after two o'clock, the second thing happened that bothered Marvin. He knew for a fact that the cafeteria staff did not show up until after three, but there in the hallway was the unmistakable smell of cooking meat. Marvin stopped and sniffed suspiciously then shook his head. *Probably some kind of breakfast meeting they have to prepare for.*

Chapter 52 - Claire

Claire was at the house project, where things had turned the corner. The house had been stripped of lath and plaster and moved to the new foundation. There had been a delay on the electricity hookup while she waited for the inspector, but now the wiring was approved, the plumbing hooked up, and the drywall in place. Dust was not an issue, so John was in a carrier on her back while she did a walk-through, admiring the progress and planning the next stages, while John Returns From Hunt was out picking up some drywall compound. Alone in the house, upstairs she heard the squeak of the front stairs. John must have made the trip in record time.

"Pretty fast, hey, kiddo?" She reached back to chuck little John on the chin.

But the man who entered the room was not John but some guy in dark-gray coveralls, new leather work gloves, and the kind of soft-soled work boots that made little noise. He had a medium-sized crowbar in his hand.

"Who are you?"

The guy said nothing, just moved to her left a little to block the exit to the stairs.

Claire felt her hackles rise. She wheeled around and sprinted through the back doorway to the rear of the house. The house she was renovating was typical of the style and period of the time and had two stairways, one in front for the family and a smaller one in the back for the servants. The latter was the staircase she headed for, making the top of the stairs about three steps ahead of the stranger with the crowbar. She hit the second floor, landing where a hallway to the bedrooms on the second floor split off.

Keep going down the stairs, or head to the front of the house? The trip to the front of the house was longer but could be seen from the street. If she took the stairs, the pickup was in back, a possible escape.

She headed down the hallway, arms pumping, feet driving, Little John jouncing. Suddenly, she heard an enormous crash intermingled with a bellow of fury. Turning, she could see John Returns From Hunt staring angrily down the staircase at something she couldn't see. "John? You okay?"

He turned and slowly deflated down into his normal self. Claire walked quickly back and looked down the staircase. At the bottom was a huge dent in the drywall, the two-by-fours broken. Carefully, Claire went down the stairway to examine the damage. A bloody piece of scalp and hair was stuck in a broken two-by-four, a small dot of blood and the crowbar off to the side.

Again, she asked, "You okay?"

John nodded.

"What happened?"

John shrugged. "I threw him."

Adrenaline was kicking in, making her knees weak and her heart race. She leaned against the door and then felt the need to sit on the steps, laughing weakly with relief. "Well, I hope you hurt him."

"Who is he?"

"No idea."

"He try to hurt you and John?" John started to swell up, an angry grizzly bear again.

"No, no, we're good, John. Sure glad you came back early." Suddenly puzzled, Claire asked, "So why did you come back so fast? I thought for sure you'd be gone an hour."

John gave the baby in the backpack a strange look. "It's like he told me to."

Chapter 53 - Dean Ebert

Things were slow at the Radio Shack, and Dean was out back for a smoke break when he heard the electronic beeper at the front. He pulled a quick drag and flicked the butt, exhaling as he entered the store through the back way.

"Hey, folks, can I help you?"

There were four of them, two rangy guys in cowboy hats and boots and a hot athletic-looking chick with curly dark hair and white teeth, with a baby in a backpack.

"Nope," one of the cowboys answered as both of them grabbed coaxial cable, connectors, camera equipment, and the like. They obviously knew what they were doing, and normally, Dean would have let them at it, but the woman was the kind of looker who seldom came into a Radio Shack, so Dean decided to offer the best in customer service.

"Looks like your friends here are helping you out with a little project."

The woman was examining a VHS deck. "How long will this machine record?"

Dean reached for a bundle of tapes. "You looking at some surveillance stuff? These here 3M tapes are made for that kind of work. You can record for twenty-four hours before you need to either swap in another tape or rewind."

The little kid on her back was staring at him. Strange little kid, with no expression to speak of.

Maybe she's a babysitter. "This your little tyke?"

"Yes, sir."

Dang it. Dean didn't like little kids, but a woman like that might make him start. The cowboys were stacking stuff at the counter, and Dean's window of opportunity was shutting down fast.

"One of these fellas your husband?"

One cowboy answered for her. "Nope."

The other cowboy chimed in, "Cousins."

Some currency was on the counter, and reluctantly, Dean walked back to the till to ring the purchase. He was trying to think of witty patter, something clever and charming, but by the time he got to the till and looked up, the chick and the baby were gone, and it was just the two cowboys. *Dang it.*

He gave the change and tried to get a little sympathy vote. "So, your cousin… she married?"

Both cowboys looked at him with a hint of humor. One hefted the load of stuff in his arms. The other grabbed the bag of cables and connectors and said, "Yep."

Chapter 54 - Deidre Hall

"What happened to *you?*" Deidre pretended to be shocked and alarmed by the scrapes and bruises on Lester LaFave, but mostly, she was interested.

The pain of others fascinated her. When she was still a nurse, she would often hang around the emergency room and watch, sometimes probing and poking, just to see the reaction. She did the same to Lester. His right eye was swollen almost shut, and there was a nasty scrape across the top of his forehead into his hairline.

She took a washcloth and leaned into Lester's black eye until he yelped. "Does that hurt?"

"Whaddaya think? Ow!" Lester pulled away suddenly, holding his left arm. "Shit!"

Shushing him, Deidre coaxed him into getting out of the clothes he was in, partly to see what was damaged, partly to keep him under her control, and mostly to see what kind of pain he was in and what kind of pain he could be put in. When he was down to his underwear, she could see black-and-blue marks up and down the left arm, a large and nasty bruise on his left thigh, and some swelling in his left elbow and knee. No wonder he was limping when he'd walked in.

"Does this hurt?"

"OW! What the fuck?"

"Hush, honey. Harrison won't be home for a while, but we still should be careful." She said it in a way that made Lester aroused despite his injuries. "So... what happened to the other guy?"

LaFave barked a short laugh. "You think one guy could do this? Shit, I was teaching some punk in a motorcycle jacket a lesson in respect when three of his buddies jumped me from behind. Cocksuckers. You know that bar downtown, Skellys? I had him up on the roof for a little privacy and was tossing him down into the dumpster when these three pricks came behind and gang rushed me. I ducked the one and tossed him over my shoulder off the roof then laid a throat chop on the other, but the third got me. I lost my balance and fell onto the street."

"Oh, baby! No wonder you're bruised."

"Ow! Shit, that hurts!"

"Sorry, hon." Deidre bit her lip and leaned closer. "Hey, Lester... you still gonna be able to help me with Harrison, like we talked about? I'm scared to death."

Lester winced and gave her a game smile. "Listen, doll, if I can take care of four bikers, I can take care of one pussy surgeon."

"Okay, honey. And can you take care of one more little thing for me right now?"

"You got it, baby. Ready, willing, and able—ow! Holy shit, take it easy! Ow!"

Chapter 55 - Matt Bradley

The meeting with Stan Martin was brief. "One story of malpractice is not really a story—it's a statistical reality. A *cover-up* of malpractice is a story."

"But he's named Hall! The same name as the hospital!"

Stan looked at Matt a long minute. "You run that story, and it will look like you're picking on a guy who had a bad day."

"A bad day that messed up some poor old lady!"

"And a story that will be explained away by the hospital and, more importantly, by our audience—like I say, he will be seen as a famous guy, born with a silver spoon in his mouth, who had a bad day." Stan raised his hand before Matt could protest. "Listen, there is a bigger story here. Can't you feel it?" He steepled his fingers and started ticking off items. "First, we have a fifth-generation surgeon with a famous name. What are the odds that every single generation of the Hall family happens to be gifted in surgery? Second, we have pride. What fifth-generation family, regardless of the business, will admit that there is a dud in the family tree? Third, we have nepotism, which means fourth, we have jealousy. Every organization I've ever seen has an unofficial pecking order where everyone knows who the best are and who the worst are, and that goes for teachers, lawyers, cops, mechanics, and especially doctors. If any one of those jumps the order because of their last name, it will be the biggest sore spot and the most common thing to bitch about around the watercooler."

Matt sighed, frustrated.

This made Stan lean forward. "Listen! I'm not yelling at you—I'm encouraging you. This is going to be the biggest story this radio station ever breaks. I just need you to land the whole thing."

"How'm I gonna go that?"

Stan smiled grimly. "Find the watercooler."

Chapter 56 - Wes Cole

The day was done, the sun had sunk in the west, and there was a nip in the air that was definitely fall. Wes Cole sat on the steps of the house Claire had bought and mostly renovated. The work building the radio station was done, so he and his brother Cal had helped with some of the finish work inside the house and the rougher landscaping outside. If the truth be told, it made sense to be leaving. Wes had a small circle of friends and was comfortable with that. His closest friend and confidant was Cal. Together, they wandered around the country, answering the call of the open road with a job at the end of it.

This Sioux Falls was an eastern city, Wes figured, and a little too crowded for his taste—a sentiment echoed by Cal, who, out of the blue one day, answered Wes's unspoken thought by saying, "We'll go west next."

They probably wouldn't have come to Sioux Falls in the first place except they liked radio work and they greatly liked their cousin Claire. Claire was not her real name, but it was close enough. She'd had a tough childhood and a tougher patch after that but was still a lot like the girl who used to babysit them back in the day, a girl who took them on horseback rides and told them bedtime stories and, cousin or not, was their first crush growing up.

The radio work was mostly finished. It was time to move on, but Wes did not yet have the yearning to move, and neither did his brother. Cal had an admiration for Claire's husband, Stan, a small, intense man with piercing eyes like sunlight off an ocean.

Cal had been watching the station staff at work and would comment at night, often with a chuckle, "They are one brand to ride for."

Wes would shake his head and grin. "Yep."

As for Wes, he liked their little tyke, John. Sober as a judge, he would stare up at Wes for minutes on end. Wes would miss holding him for sure. *Something about that kid...*

Cal came out of the house with two beers, handed one to Cal, and sat on the broad concrete railing of the porch. They sat in silence for a full twenty minutes, watching the last of the season's lightning bugs and listening to the crickets and far-off traffic.

Wes cleared his throat. "We could stay on a bit, till spring, say. Maybe help Claire on the house till it's all the way done. I'd kinda like to see what Stan does with that radio station. Kinda fun."

Cal stood up, went inside, and came back with two more beers. Sitting down, he set the lip of the beer bottle on the lip of the concrete. With a gentle thump, he knocked the cap off the bottle, and he took a long sip. He belched and finished the conversation. "Yep."

Chapter 57 - Harriet Winkler

Harriet pulled off her surgical mask, blew out a sigh, and plopped down in the Hall-Hauptmann break room, checking the clock as she sat. *Five hours!*

Jane Brewster was already there, eating a yogurt. "Hard day, huh?"

"Five freaking hours for an ankle plate? You gotta be kidding me!"

Jane shrugged. "You got ol' Amblin' Al. Whaddaya expect?" Orthopedic surgeon Dr. Alan C. Selby was known to take his sweet time in surgery, a fact that miffed the staff, but what could you do about it?

Harriet checked the board to confirm her suspicions. "Great. I gotta get scrubbed and ready by two forty-five for a leg pin in OR3. That means twenty minutes, tops, to eat." Grumbling, she heaved her aching back out of the chair and opened the fridge. *Tuna fish and whole wheat.*

"Hey, Jane, you got some change for the machine? I'm gonna need more than this sandwich."

Jane handed her some change. "Knock yourself out. If you want a Coke, the machine's out."

"Nah. Snickers is what I need. I'll get some water from the cooler."

She fed the vending machine and watched the Snickers drop. "They're making them smaller all of the time." She fished the bar out and frowned. *Oh well.* Turning to the watercooler, she saw that it was empty. "Oh, great. Perfect."

Jane looked up from her novel. "What?"

"Now we're outta water."

"No. Lookit." Jane pointed. A guy was just heading into the room with two five-gallon bottles, carrying them by the necks.

"Just in time, buddy." Harriet was not joking.

The guy set the bottles down, tucked in his shirttail, and leaned against the door frame. "Sorry. New route. This the nurses' break room?"

"Sure is, pal. Unload that bottle. I need a drink." Harriet pointed to where the cooler was.

The guy hefted the bottle easily and shuffled over to the cooler. "I gotta deliver some of these to the…" He consulted a piece of paper. "Cafeteria. Main level. But they don't want it till three. Mind if I eat my lunch here?"

Jane looked at him. He was a rumpled guy, more like a kid, with beat-up tennis shoes and a gloomy face.

"Sure. Make yourself at home."

The kid plopped down at the small circular break table facing the surgical scheduling board. He fished out a crumpled brown paper sack. "Thanks."

Chapter 58 - Stan

Stan was looking at the balance sheet that Doris had printed out. He shook his head. "What's it mean?"

Doris had her own copy and was sitting across the table. "It means you're losing money."

Stan smiled wryly. "I don't need a balance sheet to tell me that. And by *me*, you mean Charlie Hofer."

Doris nodded. "Not as bad as I thought, really. Most businesses need three years to make their first dollar. You might be clear by the end of the year."

"Donnie?"

Doris rolled her eyes. "Donnie. That guy can sell Spandex to a spinster."

"I honestly never thought this place could make a go of it without Charlie's cash. Too labor-intensive. But it might. You think Charlie would stick around for that?"

"For what?" Doris asked.

"For long enough to see if KCAH can make a profit? Maybe to own it, like a regular profitable business?"

Doris scoffed. "Nope. Charlie started this radio station project for one reason only—to get even. I bet he has a list of all the members of the Oaks and is carefully marking down all the dirt you find on them. And when all the dirt is found, he'll say, 'Screw them, and screw you.' He will drop this station like a worn-out whore and go find someone else to ruin."

There was truth in Doris's words and bitterness too. Stan didn't know what to say. After a pause, she lifted her head and found the words for him.

"But I'll tell you something." She set her jaw. "Charlie don't have a corner on vengeance. There's more than one that can play at that game."

Chapter 59 - Charlie Hofer

Charlie Hofer read the KCAH morning news with glee. Reading news printed out from a radio station, sent to your computer daily, was amazing. Stan Martin was worth twice what Charlie was paying him, three times even. He'd bought a radio station because that was the only thing he could buy. The way Martin had figured out to send out stories on a computer was genius. Charlie liked to sleep in late, and printing out the morning news to read at his leisure was the greatest pleasure of his day.

Better yet, this morning's news added another name to Charlie's hit list: "Sampson Sanitary Service Accused of Collusion in Neighborhood Contracts."

Charlie pursed his lips and followed the story with a grim smile. Apparently, Sampson had approached other haulers in a scheme to divide the city into sections, removing competition and allowing for higher rates. The unnamed source suggested that this added a good ten percent to each citizen's garbage bill, and no, Sandra Sampson could not be reached for comment.

Charlie crowed loud and long, reaching for his hit list. *There... Kevin and Sandra Sampson, board members of the Oaks.* The piece of paper had eight lines drawn through it. *Not bad at all for a few months' work.*

"So long, assholes!"

So far, his premise that all the stuck-up jerks at the Oaks were crooked was not only cynical but also accurate. At this rate, every hypocritical-snob member of that place would be cast down into the mud. The thought made his one-sided smile wider.

If Doris had still been there, it would have been perfect. Frowning, Charlie poured more bourbon into his morning coffee. *Ungrateful bitch.* He'd reached out to her a few weeks back, offering to let her come home—a generous offer for sure—and she had the gall to hang up on him. Then he tried to get Stan to fire her from the radio station, and Stan Martin had hung up on him. *Ungrateful prick. Well, those two can wait. Everyone will get paid.*

Chapter 60 - Stan

Stan's eyebrows were raised. "So when I said to find out the watercooler talk, you actually went to find a watercooler?"

Matt Bradley shrugged and adjusted his glasses then went through the routine Stan was used to—he stood up, tucked in his pants, adjusted his glasses again, and settled into the door frame like he was bracing for a sou'wester. "My Uncle Dave has the Culligan dealership. He's always looking for help, so I asked if I could take the hospital."

"And?"

"You were right—they talk a lot. They have a dry-erase board in the break room, with lists of operating suites, docs, and nurses."

"See anything?"

Matt heaved a sigh and fished for a notebook in his pants pocket. "There's a list of docs, and I started writing down all the initials then checked the hospital directory to see who is who. I figure the busier docs are the better docs."

Stan shrugged. *Maybe.*

"Guess which surgeon had the least amount of surgeries? H-5."

"You think that stands for Hall the Fifth?"

Matt sighed again. "So I find out what this Hall doc operates on—hips mainly. I start asking, on behalf of my aunt Gretchen, which doc I should try to have do her hip replacement. They all say, 'Try Andresen. He's good.' Then I ask about Dr. Hall the Fifth, and they all get uncomfortable and say, 'He's good too,' but then as I'm leaving, one of the nurses says, 'I'd go with Andresen.' And she says it like it's a secret tip at a racetrack."

Stan felt the tingle up his spine that happened when a story started to pull at him. "That's not proof. You need a source."

Matt nodded glumly. "Yeah, so my cousin Ty works at the Coachlite, a dive bar that some nurses hang out at. I told him to keep an eye out for something out of the ordinary. He called me yesterday, said two nurses were deep into the Long Islands, talking loud about a cover-up, so I got over there." Matt made it sound like he'd strolled down the street, though Stan knew him enough to know that many traffic laws had been broken. "And he's right. Two nurses—a gas-passer guy and a chick—both freaking out about that nurse that's gone missing."

Stan nodded. The sister of a woman named Janet Brecht had called the station, worried enough to make it a story, not just a police report. Janet been gone one week, and there was no sign of her.

"Guess they were part of the same surgical team. You wanna guess who the surgery was for?"

Stan waited.

"Remember that doc out of the Cities and his aunt with the hip? One and the same."

Stan blew out his breath slowly, thinking. "Malpractice cover-up. You'll need more than one circumstance. Like I said, accidents happen."

It was then that Stan learned that young Matt Bradley would be an excellent poker player. Sighing, Matt adjusted his eyeglasses, revealing a spark of triumph underneath the gloom. "Yeah, but the gas passer swears that the surgery wasn't done by the surgeon. It was done by the sales rep."

Stan leaned back and whistled long and low. *Royal flush.*

Chapter 61 -Doris Tschetter

At Doris's new job at the radio station, she worked eight to five, weekdays, and had the weekends off, the polar opposite of how she'd spent the prior twenty years. As a bar waitress and stripper, her work hours had been every weekend, through the nights, with her driving home as the sun came up. She liked her new job and for the first time in her life could see a future that didn't end in shame and disgrace. But old habits were hard to break, and many weekends, she would get in her car and drive. At first, it was just aimless interstate driving, with cruise control set and the mile markers clicking by. Then one night, on impulse, she took the exit west of Oacoma, where a billboard said, Good Times at Goodies! The girl on the sign smiled seductively. She wore a sequined halter top positioned strategically behind the two *O*s in Goodies. Doris did not know the girl but felt a kinship. Dollars to donuts, she had a similar backstory to Doris and was facing the same grind—long nights, little sleep, grimy dollar bills, and pawing hands.

The paved road turned north and ended. A neon sign pointed a quarter of a mile north to more neon on a large ramshackle shed just outside of city limits and building codes. She followed the sign and pulled into the back parking lot then sat in her car, doors locked and nerves strung tight.

Not sure why she was there, she was about to put the car in reverse and back out when she saw the back door open and a woman walk out to the dumpster with a plastic bag. Without a look left or right, the woman lifted the lid and tossed the bag in. The steel lid clanged shut. The back door opened again, revealing a quick flash of neon and bar noise, then closed.

The familiarity of the scene startled Doris as she remembered the date. *First of the month.* She checked the clock on the dash. *One o'clock in the morning. We used to do the same thing in Beresford.*

She drummed the steering wheel thoughtfully, thinking about all the Goodies up and down the interstate. *Charlie.*

"Charlie." This time she said it out loud. The longer she was away from Charlie, the meaner and more pathetic she realized he was. And predictable. When she thought about it, she realized it was no surprise that he would handle his business the same way at all of his locations. And when she thought about it more, she knew it would be no surprise if he was not done with her. His meanness had a staying quality, and Doris would not be surprised at all if he was hatching some scheme against Stan Martin too. Stan was everything Charlie was not, and Charlie hated him for it. She drummed her fingers on the wheel, thinking.

Then she opened the car door and walked quickly to the dumpster. She reached inside, fished out the plastic bag, and walked briskly back to her car. Once inside, she opened the bag to confirm its contents. She checked the time—1:20. There was another Goodies up by Forestburg, on the way to Huron, about an hour and a half away.

What the heck, it's only sleep.

Chapter 62 - Barbara Hanson

Barbara Hanson was officially the head of hospital records at Hall-Hauptmann Hospital, but her nickname was Stonewall, and she was proud of it. For twenty-one years, she'd been the person that complaints, pending litigation, bill clarification, insurance claims, and more went through. She was less than five feet tall and a hundred pounds, but on the phone, she was a thousand-pound grizzly.

She was at her desk, looking at the blinking light. The person calling was a reporter from that new radio station, KCAH. *Game on.*

"Hello, medical records, this is Barbara. How may I help you?" There was no irony in her voice.

The reporter started in on his questions, and one by one, she answered them.

"I'm sorry, sir, that type of question would need to be answered by the surgeon who handled the surgery...

"I'm sorry, sir, that type of information is privileged between patient and doctor...

"I'm sorry, sir, all records pertaining to the patient you mentioned would be filed in our records office and unavailable even to me...

"No, I'm sorry, the list of surgeries handled by doctors is also privileged information...

"Yes, sir. I believe all surgeries have attending nurses and other health professionals, but I am not a doctor, and I can't confirm the nature of what those teams look like and what personnel are required for each procedure...

"No, sir, I do not know that information. No, sir, I cannot tell you who would have that information...

"Salespeople? No, sir. There *are* experts representing some of our suppliers, but no salespeople are allowed in surgery...

"I have no way of knowing what suppliers have representatives. No, sir, I don't know who would know that...

"I'm sorry, sir. We would have no records of people who are not directly employed by the hospital...

"Yes, sir. A complete directory of all doctors is available in our annual staff directory. I'm sorry, sir. I do not have a copy for distribution...

"I *am* the manager, sir. You could try any of our other staff members, but they would transfer you to me, I'm sure...

"Barbara Hanson. No, I am terribly sorry, but I have no comment at this time for any of your questions. No, I'm sorry. I cannot not share that information with you either...

"Well, I'm sorry about that—I really am. Thank you for calling, sir, and if you have any other questions that I can answer, please feel free to call. Have a nice day."

Barbara disconnected the line and smiled. Whatever that reporter was looking for he'd have to get some other way.

Chapter 63 -Sophie Holmberg

Sophie Holmberg answered the phone from her den. "Hello, Holmberg and Associates."

When things were flush, Holmberg and Associates had actually had associates, an office downtown, and even a receptionist, but that was when she'd had a chain of hospitals needing cardiologists, oncologists, pediatric doctors, and more. Then they decided to handle things in-house, and they tossed her to the curb.

Oh well. Quickly, Holmberg had pivoted into a side business, handling medical equipment sales and hunting reps looking for bigger commissions and better territories, and she'd cut her own staff to tide her over. Now she was solo, with ads in every Yellow Pages in the Midwest, like a fisherman with a hundred lines in the water, waiting for a nibble. This call was one of those nibbles, a question about Sioux Falls, South Dakota.

"Sioux Falls? Nice town!" Sophie had driven through Sioux Falls once on the way to Denver and used that as her guide. "You looking to move there?"

She pulled a pad of paper and started jotting things down.

"Uh-huh. Uh-huh. Divorce, huh? Yeah, too bad. Kids moved there? Yeah, well you gotta be there for 'em, that's for sure." The guy sounded kind of glum. The divorce might explain that.

She wrote down the word *sales* and underlined it twice.

"So, how much experience, do you have? Fifteen years? Good. Have you got a résumé, stats of sales, growth, etcetera?"

She nodded furiously, reaching for the Sioux Falls file out of the file cabinet.

"Yeah, you betcha. It's a growing market, that's for sure. Hall-Hauptmann is the biggest medical provider between Mayo and Denver. What's your line?"

She started jotting down names—Hillenbrand, Stryker, Olympus, Zeiss. Quite a list. It looked like the guy had job-hopped his way up to Chicago before the wife dumped him. *Oh well.*

"Yeah, well, hang on a sec. There's a couple three possibilities might be good for you. There's a guy retired outta optical equipment. He had a big territory, lots of potential. Some guy went AWOL out of Panco, left a really nice list behind, and a hotshot ortho who was the team doc for the Niners has some new patented stuff. It's a start-up, but I got a feeling…"

The caller asked a question.

"Panco… that's right! And poof! He disappeared. Panco's got a full line—ankles to skull plates and everything in between. You get a guy who wipes out on his motorcycle on the way to Sturgis, and you can take a month off!"

They both laughed appreciatively.

"Yeah, an ill wind, huh?" She checked the name on the Panco file. "Nope. It wasn't Harris. The guy's

name is Devon LaCroix. He musta just freaked out.
Some guys'll do that. Don't know a good thing when
they have it. Look," Sophie said, closing the deal.
"I've been doing this for eighteen years. You can try
another rep, maybe even try Panco. But I know the
territory, and I know what they'll pay, so let me rep
for you, and I'll get you a fee you deserve at a place
near your kids."

She wrote the guy's name down—Matt Bradley—
and tossed it in the thirty-day file. Follow-ups were
key.

Chapter 64 - Stan Martin

There were four of them in the back booth of the Coachlite. Stan Martin was doing most of the talking, Matt Bradley was doing most of the listening, and the other two were doing most of the drinking.

"My name is Stan Martin. I am the general manager of KCAH radio, a station whose format is news based with an interest in investigative journalism. What my associate has uncovered is shocking." He nodded to Matt. "We have proof of a surgeon who needs to leave the profession, circumstantial evidence of an unauthorized person performing surgery, a hospital that aided in a cover-up, and the suspicious disappearance of two people who were in the same operating room you were in." Stan continued, "We do not need to mention your names. You will continue to be sources protected by qualified privilege for confidential information under state law. I personally believe that this story needs to be aired for the good of the community but also to protect you. The fact that two people are missing seems suspicious to me."

The two across the table said nothing, but they reached for their drinks simultaneously and drained them dry. Sean, a handsome guy with bags under his eyes and a two-day stubble, took a shuddering breath. He looked like he hadn't slept for a week. He nodded at the equally haggard woman to his left.

"So, Ann and Janet and I were in the OR, waiting for a hip surgery with Dr. Hall, the one they call Five…"

"Wait a sec." Stan pushed the record button on the tape deck. "Okay, start again."

The two leaned over the table and, in hushed tones, told their story.

Chapter 65 - Everett Meyer

Everett Meyer, senior council for Hall Media and senior partner at Lammi, Luehmann, Meyer, and Otto, was a man of luxurious habits. Rising early, he would take a porcelain cup of black coffee, a fresh scone from Brenda's Bakery, and the morning issue of the *Plains Beacon*. Dressed in a freshly pressed shirt and suit with braces, he would sit at the breakfast nook next to the patio and survey the news of the day. In the winter, the French doors to the patio were closed. In the summer and fall, he would open the French doors and enjoy his breakfast in the garden.

In the last six months, he'd made two distinct changes to this ritual, one a pleasure, the other a pain. The first had to do with the paper. He'd heard from a colleague that ironing a newspaper set the ink into the paper and prevented ink smudges. He'd had the morning maid start ironing the paper ever since. It was a tactile pleasure to hold the crisp, warm paper in his hands as he worked his way through its contents. This morning the maid—he thought her name was Paulina—was fussing with the paper. *How hard can it be to iron it?* She had two of the pages in the wrong order. Exasperated, Meyer sorted the paper himself. *Oh well.*

The pain had to do with what the paper didn't have—news. Oh, maybe it was harsh to say, but the buzz around town usually had nothing to do with the paper but, instead, what was heard on the new radio station, KCAH. This was irritating for a number of reasons. The first was that the owner, Charlie Hofer, an odious, loathsome creature who owned a number of strip clubs in the state and who hired a fleet of attorneys for healthy fees, always in conflict with the needs and desires of Hall Media Group. For that reason, Meyer was never privy to those fat legal fees. The second irritating reason was that Hall Media would never lower itself to repeating the news reported by KCAH on their more robust signals, so he was forced to search out its staticky signal.

Other friends and colleagues simply took the email version of the news and had it sent to their home or office, an option that seemed disloyal to Meyer, especially if he was caught. So now, each morning, Meyer had a deadline. He had to finish breakfast and the paper, get dressed for the office, and be out of the garage and down the road by six thirty to catch the station on his car radio. The station's actual signal was so weak he couldn't hear it from his dining room, but the Mercedes sound system was excellent, and he could motor through town and listen to the first morning-news broadcast in surround-sound clarity.

On that particular Monday morning, Meyer turned north off of Fifty-Seventh Street onto Minnesota Avenue just as the news sounder played. Traffic was light, and he coasted down the hill toward the river and into town. Meyer adjusted the volume. He felt a little schadenfreude as he listened to the news of what others had been caught doing, giving a silent chuckle at the confirmation of a rumor or genuine surprise about a scandal.

Gretchen Wallace was the morning announcer. Meyer had to admit, he loved her delivery. She had a well-modulated voice—never hurried, with hints of humor, irony, or warmth depending on the nature of the story she was reading. Meyer knew for a fact that KCAH had only four working reporters besides her, not including Stan Martin, but they must have been hardworking because the amount and variety of dirt they were able to uncover was impressive.

"Good morning. This is Gretchen Wallace reporting from the C, M, and G Railroad studios, with the morning report. Our headline this morning covers accusations by trusted sources of a botched surgery at Hall-Hauptmann Hospital. Our investigation reveals that an unlicensed nonmedical contractor performed a routine procedure that resulted in irreversible damage and a subsequent cover-up that reaches to the highest levels of the hospital. Investigative reporter Matt Bradley will file his report, following this message from Arthur's Shoes."

Meyer's heart stopped. *Shit*. Too soon, the commercial was over, and the deadpan delivery of Matt Bradley laid out the details of Harrison Benjamin Hall's operating debacle with alarming accuracy. Meyer's morning commute was no longer quiet or relaxing. He had a lot of work to do that day, and many heads were going to roll. And it was very important that one of those heads was not his.

Chapter 66 - Lester LaFave

Lester LaFave had seen *The Godfather* at least four times. His favorite scene was the horse head. He'd often wondered how they did that part—if they killed a real horse just for the movie or got one from a horse that was going to die anyway or if it was a fake. Anyway, he remembered enough about it to learn the importance of intimidation—getting to a guy when he was off guard and vulnerable. At work, they were ready for trouble. At home, they were relaxed, safe. That was the place and time to mess with their heads or maybe mess with more than their heads.

Stan Martin was making waves, creating little messes that needed to be cleaned up. LaFave saw himself as a cleaner—a simple, passionless cleaner who got rid of messes. Except maybe for that asshole Indian. He'd like to play a little catchup with that fucker. *Tune him up a little. Make him bleed. Try out some of his toys.*

LaFave had asked for and gotten all of the stuff he thought he might need based on all the crime shows he'd seen—anonymous coveralls, pantyhose for his face, a cattle prod, and some guns. He had no idea what kind of gun he might need, so he'd asked for a shotgun—he sawed off the barrel himself, just like Charles Bronson did—a 22 with a silencer, and a Colt 1911. He was going to ask for a Walther PK, like James Bond used, but decided to stick with American made.

The plan was simple: take a Hall Cable TV truck for cover, walk in, and blast a kneecap off of the first man, woman, or child he saw. Then write "Vulnerable" in lipstick on a wall somewhere. Red lipstick, impossible to trace. Nothing fancy. Then he'd dump the gun and the shoes—sometimes they could use shoe imprints to find people—in the Big Sioux River, park the truck in the back of the cable station, and strip off the coveralls. He had a pair of navy slacks and gray cashmere sweater underneath, loafers in the van. He'd switch back over to his car, looking like Robert Mitchum in *The Big Sleep*, only meaner. Philip Marlowe on the outside, Don Corleone on the inside.

LaFave smiled. *Show time.*

Chapter 67 - Everett Meyer

Law was more than just rules on paper. Ultimately, law was the sense of right versus wrong, and that was a nuanced thing. Shaping and manipulating that nuance was what Meyer did very well. The first point went to him. He had the meeting at his office on the second floor, giving him home-field advantage with his leather chairs, mahogany panels, and professional staff of disdainful legals and paralegals who had to be walked through like a gauntlet.

The second point went to him as well. A Sioux Falls police detective and a district head of the Federal Communication Commission were on hand as a favor to him. Certainly, laws had been broken at the municipal level. Meyer had some building codes researched. There was a chance he could raise a stink about the placement of KCAH offices, which wasn't in the purview of the detective, of course, but having him at the table would make Martin and his cronies nervous. As far as the FCC was concerned, Meyer was on more solid ground. Using a front like Emilio Gonzales to start what was purported to be a Spanish religious station, thereby sneaking around the FCC guidelines, was shady at best, and having the FCC representative at the table offered a third point, a moral high ground that would give Meyer an even greater advantage at the meeting.

The meeting was scheduled for ten o'clock in the morning. Meyer had Martin's group wait outside until 10:35. Finally, a frosty receptionist Meyer used to make visitors feel inferior showed the guests in. Along with Martin came a big shuffling kid named Matt Bradley. Meyer vaguely recognized him from a report on all of the employees of KCAH, and he remembered that Bradley had once worked for Hall Media. The third person was a kid named Ray Crew. Meyer knew only a little bit about him. He was a farm kid with a law degree from the University of South Dakota, who worked for Charlie Hofer. Hofer hired him because he was cheap, and Crew took the job because it was the only one he could find out of law school.

There were six chairs on his side and three across from them. Meyer made sure the three were a little lower, making his guests look like grade schoolers invited to the adult table. *Easy peasy.*

Meyer's stock in trade was a smooth delivery with sharp unexpected jabs, and while the three across the table were getting themselves comfortable, he laid out his first punch. "Slander." He tossed three heavy files across the table like hand grenades. "Untrue accusations made on your radio station, by you, Mr. Martin, inflicting irreparable damage to my client."

He tossed another three salvos. "Libel. Continued lies, distributed through email, that once printed meet the definition of libel. You, Mr. Bradley, have fallen in with a bad crowd and now must pay the price for your foolish decision. You personally will be sued, and by the time I am done with you, you won't be able to get a job delivering pizzas. And you, Mr. Martin…"

Meyer leveled his gaze on the smaller man next to Bradley, a fairly anonymous-looking guy with a spare frame and startlingly intense eyes. "You are in…"

"Stop." Martin said the word with command, and Meyer found himself momentarily speechless. Martin rose and leaned on the table. "You, Mr. Meyer, are a well-paid attorney, well worth the money you make." He nodded to the other five. "And you all may or may not be privy to Mr. Meyer's strategies." He pointed to the door. "Making us wait for thirty-five minutes. Having us sit in chairs three inches lower than yours. Simple little games that are designed to make us feel small—intimidation that I have felt before as a member of the press. So let us stop the games and put our cards on the table." Martin motioned to Bradley, who took a tape recorder out of a box. "We altered the voices, but here is an excerpt of the interview given."

Five minutes later, Martin stopped the tape. Meyer tried bluster. "That is a fabrication… taken out of context."

"No doubt vetted completely when you decide to take us to trial, Mr. Meyer. A trial we will cover, of course," Martin said.

"If you expect the fine people of this city to believe the likes of that sleaze monger, Charlie Hofer, and your staff of boozers, strippers, and misfits…"

"Be careful, Mr. Meyer," the erstwhile quiet Crew said. "Charlie Hofer is the owner of KCAH, and he owns a chain of strip clubs, which are legal businesses in the state of South Dakota. Mr. Martin is a recovering alcoholic, also common knowledge, also not illegal, and also the reality of, no doubt, many other employees all over the state, probably even at Hall Media. No laws have been broken by my clients. None."

The detective from the police department looked at Meyer, waiting for a response.

Meyer fished out a document. "If Mr. Hofer is the owner of the station, why does this application refer to Emilio Gonzales as the owner?"

Crew held his hands out and shrugged. "It is common for owners to use holding companies as a way to separate themselves from various business practices. It's legal, especially when it pertains to the intent of the federal regulations—allowing a diverse and differing opinion in the local community. KCAH may not be Spanish speaking or religious, but it does offer a different voice in this community, one that many have applauded and many listen to." Crew gave a disarming smile. "Adding to the numbers of reporters and news gatherers in a community is a good thing."

The FCC official looked at Meyer, also waiting. Meyer's mind raced, thinking of a suitable retort. In the gap, Stan motioned for Matt Bradley to reach into the box and pull out a small TV. "Speaking of illegal, I thought I might show this to you. It comes from a series of cameras around my house."

Alarm bells sounded in Meyer's mind.

"My wife was going to report it this morning, but I asked if I could borrow the tape. The original tape is much longer and in a safe place." He looked at Meyer pointedly. "But Matt was able to edit it down. By the time stamp in the corner of the recording, you can see this took place late last night while I was covering a city council meeting."

Stan plugged in the TV, slid a videocassette into the base, and hit Play. There was no sound, but the pictures were damning. An exterior shot showed a van pulling up, the words Hall Cable clearly visible on its side. A tall, muscular figure in coveralls got out of the van and walked toward a doorway.

"This is a house my wife is remodeling and we are living in. There has been some suspicious activity, so she installed these cameras."

Now the figure in the coveralls could be seen tiptoeing through the interior of the house. It looked almost ludicrous, like a black-and-white silent movie, but the gun in the hand of the figure was anything but funny. Coming into a room, the figure was visible through a distorted fish-eye lens. A crib was in a corner. Then in a flashing blur of movement, a woman wielding what looked like a golf club swung and hit a wall just above the ducking figure. There was a flash of light from the muzzle of the gun then another blow—this time, the woman jabbing the handle of the golf club into the stomach of the intruder. Then, through various camera shots, the figure could be seen running, staggering to the van, and driving off.

Stan stopped the tape. "My wife said he was wearing pantyhose over his head and gloves. He dropped his gun. She thinks it's the same person who tried to attack her before."

The detective was now fully alert. "I'll need to file a report on this. Can I talk to your wife?"

The room was abuzz with irrefutable evidence of a felony involving Hall Media property. Everyone ignored Meyer. In the past, he'd been a shield for anyone who needed legal council. For the first time in his life, Meyer found himself running through a mental list of colleagues he knew, calculating his own exposure.

Time for a scapegoat.

Chapter 68 - Harrison Hall

Harrison Hall was livid. "You incompetent fool!" He lashed out at Lester LaFave. "How could you be caught on tape, breaking into Stan Martin's home?"

"Pipe down, pal." LaFave was in the remote furnace room in the basement of the hospital, meeting with Hall and his son, Benjamin, a hasty gathering based on the evidence that Hall's lawyer Meyer had given.

It was after hours. The cinder-block room was dimly lit, the noise of the furnace almost deafening. Hall was at his wits' end, and Benjy looked scarcely better, but LaFave was sitting on the edge of a janitor's desk, calmly lighting a cigarette, cupping the flame with his hands and squinting like he was in a film noir.

"It was a setup." LaFave snapped the silver Zippo closed and pocketed it. "Martin or Hofer must have someone with eyes in this dump, someone feeding them information. I'da capped that Martin chick, one-two, but they'da had it on tape, and I'd be stamping plates at the Hill Hilton, waiting for my turn at the needle." LaFave jerked his head, motioning in the general direction of the state prison that sat on a bluff on the north side of Sioux Falls. He blew a jet of smoke out of the side of his mouth.

Hall opened his mouth and closed it. He'd seen the video. It looked like a Keystone Cops movie, the figure of LaFave running for his life, chased by a golf-club-wielding woman in a nightie. Yet here was LaFave, cracking wise like Robert De Niro or Jimmy Cagney.

"Now, you listen to me." Hall pointed a finger. "I have paid you good money on retainer for results, and nothing has happened. I told you to handle a loose end." Hall raised an eyebrow, hinting at the earlier conversation about getting rid of Deidre. "And all I'm getting in return is more of your excuses."

"Excuses." LaFave inhaled deeply then exhaled, flicking the cigarette off to the side. He looked at Benjamin. "And you? What do you think?"

Benjamin twitched awkwardly. Hall had been watching him over the past few weeks and had seen the obvious decline toward a breakdown. Yet the smugness that came with his childhood and the arrogance that came with his intelligence were still evident.

"You are a two-bit hoodlum hired to do a job and doing it badly," Benjamin said.

LaFave shrugged, resigned. "All right, lemme explain a couple things. First is, I've had to wait on capping this wife of yours until you're out of town so you're in the clear, right?"

Hall's mouth dropped open, aghast that LaFave would blab this confidence.

Benjy's mouth was open, too, and turned to his father. "You… what?"

LaFave then pulled the 22-caliber pistol from his pocket. "And the second is that while I've been down here, I've been trying to decide which of you snobby assholes annoys me the most, and, junior, it's you."

With that, LaFave fired twice into Benjamin, the sound of the shots as shocking as the blossoms of red that splashed across the younger man's chest. The horrified look on both Halls' faces remained as the younger slipped to the floor. The roar of the furnace continued, the ringing in Harrison Hall's ears, the smell of cordite, and the body of his son a ghastly abnormality in such a dull and drab place.

"There." LaFave heaved a sigh of satisfaction. "I never did like that prick. And," he added, pointing the gun at Hall, "I don't like you either, but this little deal makes us partners, see?"

He gestured to Benjamin's body on the floor. "This little murder will make for a real messy look for you and the schmancy hospital you run, huh? So I'm gonna leave, and you're gonna clean this up."

LaFave stood erect, adjusting his suit jacket and pocketing the gun. "Dump the stiff. Call me tomorrow. Tell me when and how you are leaving town, where you are staying, and when you will be back. And, buddy boy?" LaFave stepped close to Hall, looked down at him, and patted him on the cheek, leaning in. "Don't ever call me a fool."

Chapter 69 - Lester LaFave

It had taken a while to nail down, but now that he had, he felt like a million bucks. He was Robert Mitchum. Tall and tough, no-nonsense. He swaggered to Deidre's house, world-wise and confident.

"Hey, doll." He shrugged out of his jacket and into her arms.

Her kiss was hot and her eyes cool. "Well?"

"I had a little meeting with your lovely hubby and son."

"And?"

"There was a little talk about the conversation I wanted to have with the reporter Stan Martin's wife."

Deidre sighed. "You mean when you got run off by a woman with a golf club?"

LaFave was hurt. "The cops were wise to it—had to have been. Musta been a fink who ratted me out."

She rolled her eyes and shook her head disdainfully. "Did you actually just say that? You sound like one of those cheesy black-and-white movies."

Wounded, he couldn't think of something clever and settled for "I do not."

"Listen, *Lester*." She moved in and grabbed him by the jaw, digging her nails in. "What did you do?"

"Nothin'." He almost added "honest" to the sentence but bit the word off short. "I was supposed to meet with Harrison and his son, but the kid never showed."

"Why not?"

"How should I know?"

Her eyes narrowed, studying him. "What we have is an inconvenient crime, an accident really. No one wants to talk about this accident except for a small group of people. If you take care of the witnesses to the accident, assure them of the mistake of appearing in court, I can take care of the nosy few reporting on it." She stepped in closer. "And if at the same time, we solve the problem of an abusive husband, we can all have a Merry Christmas."

She grabbed the crotch of his pants and twisted, leading him to the bedroom.

Chapter 70 - Jim Fletcher

After a long week at the radio station, ag reporter Jim Fletcher was grabbing a beer and a basket of chislic at the Holiday Inn downtown. The hotel bar was perfect for Fletcher—quiet enough for him to catch some Nebraska hoops on the bar screen, cheap enough with a special on-tap beer and a waitress who was obviously flirting for tips. He sat at a table near the screen. A booth would have been more comfortable but awkward for eating by himself.

The game was a bust. The Huskers were down by twenty at the half. *Damn Sooners.*

Fletcher looked at the last inch of beer and was lifting the glass to drain it when he saw her in the mirror over the bar. Blue blazer and matching skirt with cream-colored blouse. She'd kicked off one heel and was massaging her foot. There was a bag of camera equipment on the floor next to her, and she was rummaging through it, packing a cord and mic inside. *TV reporter.*

"Anyone know the score of the game?" she asked.

Fletcher knew. "Huskers down by twenty at the half."

"Damn Sooners." She shook her head and smiled wryly. "Better stick with football."

Fletcher nodded. She had blond hair, green eyes, and a dazzling smile. She was way out of his league, but what the heck. "You a reporter?"

"Yep. KARE 11. My flight from Denver had trouble, so they routed me through here."

Fletcher nodded. KARE was out of Minneapolis. "You gonna miss a deadline?"

She shrugged. "Not too bad. It's an ag piece. Fluff for the metro audience."

"What's the piece?"

She looked at him appraisingly. "You a reporter?"

He raised his hands. "Guilty as charged."

"Where at?"

"Formerly WNAX farm reporter, now for a local news station."

"Wait a minute… are you Jim Fletcher?"

"Same."

"Gosh, my dad used to listen to you do the markets every morning! I thought I recognized your voice." She actually looked a little starstruck.

The waitress stopped by. "Ready to settle up?"

Jim decided he was terribly thirsty. "Get me another beer and some more chislic."

The reporter extended her hand. "Kendra Donnelly, KARE weekends. It's a real honor."

"Jim… well you know me, I guess." He blushed.

"So what do you do now, Jim?"

"Oh, I was hired away to do some investigative work for a local radio station, KCAH." He tried to sound important.

"Oh hoo! So you work *there*!" She scooted her chair close and started whispering. "That station is ripping it up! Our news director talks about you guys all the time." Her eyes were shining with excitement.

Jim resisted the urge to smooth his hair back. He wondered if he still had a mint in his pocket.

"So—what's the secret sauce, huh?" She poked him playfully.

"What do you mean?"

"You know, who's behind finding all those stories? I have an uncle who lives in Valley Springs. He says there's a story almost every day that's juicy."

Most of the time, Fletcher hunkered down and kept quiet when the station was talked about. There was a lot of jeering over the weak signal of a station owned by a strip-club owner and broadcast from a strip mall. But not that night. Those who appreciated journalism had to stick together.

He leaned back in his chair and shrugged a shoulder. "My opinion? Stan Martin. He came looking for me, said he wanted a solid ag department focusing on the consumer and investor, then signed me up for more than I ever made at WNAX—triple my old salary. But that's just the beginning. He took a lot of us who were kind of bored with what we were doing, got us in a room, and just started challenging us to find news."

He looked at her, wondering if he would be laughed at for what he said next. "It's… exciting. Something about the group of us, it's competitive, but it's also more than that." He lowered his voice. "That kid who broke the Hall-Hauptmann story—the botched surgery that implicates a member of the Hall family?" Fletcher shook his head. "I mean, a kid broke it. Matt Bradley is his name. But it was like we all broke it. We were all gathered around the radio monitor, listening to the story as it aired. You should have seen the phones lighting up.

"And then, about seven thirty that morning, when Stan came in, I can't describe it. We just automatically stood up—traffic, sales, all of us. Stan looked around at each one of us and then said, 'I'm very proud of you, all of you.'" Fletcher looked to see if she was smirking. "I know, cheesy, right? Sure, we bicker and fight a bit. Who doesn't? But when Stan comes in, it's all business. Never ever had a job like that before."

The girl looked thoughtful, her smile gone. "So Stan Martin is the reason you have so much success?"

"Definitely. His vision, his leadership, his encouragement. Charlie Hofer has the money, but without Stan Martin, the whole thing would fall apart—trust me."

She tapped a long, sharp fingernail on the table, *tik, tik, tik.* Her smile returned, a little thin, her voice somewhat absent. "Oh, I trust you all right."

Chapter 71 - Harrison Hall

Harrison Benjamin Hall IV was trying not to unravel. In the past few days, he'd gotten rid of two bodies, one a nurse he'd murdered, the other his own son. The emotions he thought should be there were not. No grief or remorse or even guilt, only a fear-driven manic energy, the kind that soldiers in combat must feel, waiting any second to be killed yet for the moment still alive, still fighting.

"What are you doing here?"

Harrison jumped and almost screamed, wheeling around. Deidre was walking in from the bedroom, wrapping a thin silk robe around her and tying it. Never modest, Deidre could be easily seen through the bank of windows that let in the warm sun. At other times, this would have aroused him, but now it only made him angry.

"Get some clothes on! People can see you!"

She walked by him with a tumbler of vodka, ignoring him. She sat on one of the pieces of patio furniture she'd moved inside, a teak deck chair modeled after the ones they had on the Titanic. She lay back in its arms, one naked knee jutting up out of the slit in the front of the robe, tilting her face to the sun.

Jiggling the tumbler to stir the ice, she turned her face and observed him coolly. "You look like shit, Harrison. Something bothering you?"

The drink she was holding appealed to him more than she did. Gathering himself, he ignored her, walked to the bar, and made himself a Scotch, four fingers. He drank off the top half, added three cubes, and topped it to the rim.

Then he drank a third of that and walked over to his wife, looking down at her. "You've heard the news, I imagine?"

She lifted a shoulder. "What does Benjy say?"

Harrison kept his face immobile and took another sip. "I haven't seen him."

"I don't have to tell you that the boy is weak. He should never have gone into medicine."

Hall raised his chin. "He's a Hall. Medicine is our calling."

She laughed derisively. "Medicine is your *business*. You don't care about him. You only care about your business, your precious reputation."

"And yours, my dear. All of this"—he gestured to the house and surrounding estate outside—"is because of what you call my precious business."

She looked at him and threw out a sentence, like she was testing him. "It's just a story. It'll blow over."

Hall took another sip and looked into his drink. Deidre had been livid when she'd heard the news. *Why is she so unconcerned all of a sudden?* He was tempted to ask about Devon LaCroix, the missing sales rep, but the way she seemed so relaxed made him realize that she most certainly had a hand in his disappearance. She could not know about the missing nurse or about Benjy.

Three of the eight people who had been witnesses to the surgery were dead, and the remaining five could be handled by Meyer and his lawyers. He sipped again, the liquid calming his nerves, helping him realize that he was very close to the end. Deidre did not know about LaFave, another ace up his sleeve—a psychopathic killer and liar but also alone and unattached. LaFave didn't know that Hall, too, could be violent if needed, and at the right time, he would have his vengeance for his son's murder.

My son's murder. He rolled the thought in his mind. Curious—it still did not cause any anguish. Perhaps Deidre was right, and the boy was too weak to carry the Hall name. Maybe it was better that he was gone. There was just one problem.

"Do you really think that Neanderthal Charlie Hofer will stop dragging our name through the mud?"

Deidre took a sip, touching the rim of glass with a fingertip. "Charlie Hofer is a Neanderthal and only has money. The answer is stopping the brains behind it." Her eyes did not meet his—they stayed focused on the rim of her glass—but the point was taken.

"The death of Stan Martin would cause suspicion."

"Yet accidents happen every day," she said.

"He's a radio announcer, not a coal miner. What's he supposed to do—fall off a radio tower?"

Chapter 72 - Wes

"Yoo-hoo!" The call came from outside the transmitter shack.

Wes looked at Cal, who shrugged. The tower site was three miles out of town down a gravel road and not on the way to anywhere. Wes stepped to the doorway of the shack. Brilliant sunshine on white snow made him squint against the glare. Off on the road a ways, he could see where a small SUV had slid into a ditch. Footprints led through some small drifts to the woman shivering outside the fence.

"C-Can you help me?" Her jacket was too light for the weather, and she was not wearing boots. Snow would have gotten into her shoes, no doubt.

Wes threw on his lined denim coat and cowboy hat and walked the narrow shoveled path to the gate. "You stuck?"

Already, her cheeks and nose were pink from the cold. "I s-sure am." She shivered.

"Well, come on inside and warm up a bit." Wes opened the gate and led her inside.

"Whew! Th-Thanks! It is nice and toasty in here." She was wearing one of those fur-lined blanket jackets that cinched in at the waist and stopped just above the butt. They were no good for keeping warm, especially in a wind, but they were good to look at. Cal had stopped his work and was enjoying the view.

Wes had a good view too. Her eyes were bright green, and her blond hair framed a perfect jaw and cheekbones. She looked like a model for a ski resort.

"It's the transmitter. It throws off a lot of heat." Fans around the army-green box made it seem like a furnace.

"Gosh, are those light bulbs?"

"Nope. This whole transmitter's a relic from World War II. Those are tubes that make the transmitter work. Not very efficient anymore but real cheap." Cal pointed to shelves along the wall. "We probably got enough tubes to last fifty years right there. No need for an upgrade."

"Can I sit down and get the snow out of my shoes?" She looked doubtfully at the signs that said DANGER and HIGH VOLTAGE and WARNING.

"Don't worry about that out here. That's only for behind there."

Wes pulled a metal stool around. She perched on the edge of it, took off a pair of jogging shoes, and knocked the snow off, rubbing her wet stocking feet.

"Here, turn around this way." Wes pointed to the grating at the bottom of the transmitter.

"The heat gets vented out here. Your feet will warm in no time," Cal added. Both had decided that helping this gal out and making her feel at home was their duty.

"Oh, it is *warm!*" She shed her jacket and sat on it. She was wearing a thin V-neck cashmere sweater that looked very nice. Very nice indeed. "Thanks for saving my life. It'd have been a long walk."

Both Cal and Wes nodded. That was a bit of an exaggeration. They had not saved her life, but they had saved her a long cold walk.

Cal reached for his coat. "We'll get you unstuck."

"Thanks, but I'm in no hurry. I'd just as soon warm up a bit."

They both smiled. Fine with them.

"So what is this place?" She looked around, curious.

"Radio tower site."

The shack was small, but her curiosity was large. In the course of half an hour, they told her that the tower was four hundred feet tall, almost no one except them came out to there, the fence was to protect people from touching the tower and getting electrocuted, and the heavy steel grating over the building was a bridge to catch ice falling off the tower. They answered a surprising number of other questions too.

"So that whole big tower is electrified?" she asked.

Wes nodded. "That's the way AM towers work."

"Gosh! And you climb on it?"

Cal chuckled. "Not when it's on." He pointed to the heavy throw switch that said ON-OFF. "We service it at night and shut 'er down before we climb."

"But that's four hundred feet!"

"Yes, ma'am."

"But what if you fell?"

Wes nodded. "It can happen. That's why we wear a safety harness."

"But can't the tower fall over? It looks awfully skinny."

Cal took her to the door and pointed. "It's guyed up all the way around with those wires, see? They're pulled tight on three sides and keep it from falling over."

"Gee!" She put her hand on Cal's chest to steady herself. "That makes me weak in the knees just thinking about it."

Cal was happy to help.

While her socks dried, Wes and Cal shoveled out the walkway a bit, drove their pickup out, and pulled her SUV, leaving her alone in the shack. That was technically a no-no, but it didn't make much sense to leave her out in the weather to freeze.

Chapter 73 - Charlie Hofer

Charlie Hofer sat back in his leather office chair, reading the KCAH email of the day's news, chuckling. The latest report showed that more than twenty-five hundred people were paying to have email delivered daily, and the revenues of the station were projected to break even by February. Hofer could expect to have a profitable radio station and revenue generator within sixty days.

Fuck that. Already, he'd gotten what he wanted. Almost all of the pricks at the Oaks had been dragged through the mud, not with name-calling or innuendo but with real legitimate hand-caught-in-the-cookie-jar news. He laughed again.

The best and last example was Harrison Fucking Benjamin Fucking Hall Fucking the Fifth. The snotty little prick with the snooty attitude was nowhere to be found, according to the morning's radio report. The town was abuzz, and his pompous stuffed-shirt daddy was avoiding the press.

Now he had everything he wanted. Almost everything. Doris had left him high and dry to go work for that sanctimonious prick, Stan Martin, walking out the door and never looking back. Now he only saw her when she dropped off the balance sheets once a month, plopping them on his desk and walking out. Never a word, just a look that was a mix of anger and pity. The anger he could handle. The pity he could not.

Ungrateful slut. What she really needed was to be back on the street, out of work, to see what kind of jobs were waiting for over-the-hill strippers. No, KCAH was toast. They would all be fired, the doors closed, the signal left to rot. His revenge was almost complete. All he needed was the perfect time to drop the hammer.

He shifted his weight and smiled. *Merry Christmas.*

Chapter 74 - Wes

Wes was standing behind the control board of KCAH, waiting for the station to hit the network feed at the top of the hour. One of the pots on the board was scratchy. It was no big deal to pop it off and blow out the dust before the local evening news.

Matt Bradley was at the board. He potted up the mic and hit the button, and the monitor went silent. "It's coming up on six. Twenty-three degrees and light snow. More on the ongoing investigation at Hall-Hauptmann clinic after the network news."

Wes watched the sweeping second hand on the clock. At exactly one second to six, he saw the needle on the VU meter jump. *Bip.* Then came the network sounder.

"It's all yours, Wes." Matt sounded depressed, like a poker player losing all his chips.

Gretchen Wallace had come through the door with some actualities for Matt to play. "Hey, Captain Sunshine." The staff teased Matt for his forlorn delivery. "First one's a fifteen, outcue… 'no idea this could happen here,' then roll the piece for the cop shop, and finally, we do the latest on the Hall boys. Anything new?"

"Nah…" Matt sighed. "I got a lot of *no comment*s, and there've been no return calls from Dr. Hall's wife. I guess she used to work there as a nurse."

Gretchen raised an eyebrow. "The ice queen? Stay away from her, junior."

Matt looked interested. "Yeah?"

"I'm serious. I had a college roommate that knew her back in the day. They called her the green-eyed witch—blond hair, all the curves, and collected frat boys like scalps."

Wes was done cleaning the pot and was putting it back on the board. He dropped the monitor in cue and tested it. *Clean.*

"A looker, huh?" Matt did not seem dissuaded.

"Kiddo, she'll walk up to you, flash a smile, rip out your heart, take a bite, and hand it back to you before you hit the floor."

Wes did not hear the rest of the conversation as the studio door closed behind him. He did think about the description of the girl. *Green eyes.*

Chapter 75 - Harrison Hall

Harrison Hall hung up the phone with Brenda, the company travel agent, satisfied. Yes, the condo in the Keys was available through the first week of the new year. No, the company jet was not available until after Christmas, but yes, she could arrange a direct charter flight from Sioux Falls to Miami for the twenty-third.

In two days, it would all be over. He had a strong hunch that Deidre would take care of Stan Martin—he trusted her devious ways. It was better that he knew nothing of any details. Better yet, LaFave would take care of her while he was safely out of the state. When that job was done, he'd invite him down to the Keys, where it would be simple enough to drug him and toss him overboard into the wide-open Atlantic. Deep-sea fishing was common and chartering a boat, easy. It was a case of self-defense. Like the nurse who had tried to bribe him, LaFave was threatening more than just one person—he was affecting the livelihoods of thousands of people who depended on him, and Hall could not—*would not*—let down all those employees, medical staff, and people in need of medical help.

He smiled at himself in the mirror, examining the reflection carefully. Perhaps a lift under the chin? Why not? He deserved it. *Merry Christmas.*

Chapter 76 - Cal

Not used to being in a big city, Cal had been rubbernecking in downtown Sioux Falls, looking at knickknacks, clothing, shoes, and furniture, all on display in shop windows lit up for Christmas.

One of the bars had some pool tables in the back. It was kind of fun to play a few games, drink a beer, and observe people while he waited for Wes.

The bar was dimly lit, sparsely populated, and quiet, Cal's preferred environment. He was lining up a bank shot when he heard a familiar voice. "Hey, cowboy."

He glanced over. It was Jim Fletcher the ag reporter. Normally, Cal took offense to being called cowboy around town, since in the East River part of the state, there were layers of disrespect that required correction. Not so with Jim. He simply could not keep Cal and Wes straight, so he called them both cowboy to avoid mistakes.

"Hey." Cal nodded back.

"Up for a game?"

Cal shrugged. He knew Wes's game inside and out. It might be nice to see how the ag reporter played.

Jim put in the quarters and grabbed a cue that seemed reasonably straight. Both lagged for break, Jim missing the bumper by an inch and a half. *Not bad.* Cal eyed him, wondering if there was some kind of hustle in the making. There was not. Jim's dad had run a PX in the war, and their basement had a top-of-the-line slate table in it.

"I've been shooting pool since I could barely see over the table," Jim said.

They circled the table in companionable silence, making good shots, leaving tough lays, pretty evenly matched, a good way to pass the time.

The game over, Cal looked up. "Another one?"

But Jim was distracted, watching the TV screen over the bar. It was a station out of the Cities that carried a Gophers game, and during a break, the local news team was teasing the ten o'clock news. Jim stopped and eyed the blonde on the screen. "Nope, different one." He turned to Cal. "I was over at the Holiday Inn when I talked to a gal who's a reporter there." He nodded at the screen. "Holy smoke. Made that girl look like a dishrag."

Cal gave Jim his full attention.

"Blond hair to about here. A smile like a five-hundred-watt bulb and green eyes, not to mention the dairy character… good suspensory ligaments." He winked. Jim had spent many years coaching FFA people on livestock judging and was known to apply those judging terms to women. Cal had spent some time in FFA himself and knew what Jim meant by the term.

"Green eyes?"

"Green as grass. I think she had a little thing for me," Jim confided.

Cal nodded, thinking about the woman whose SUV was stuck by the radio tower. *Small world.*

Chapter 77 - Claire

Christmas was two days away, the house was finished, and Claire was ready to give Stan the tour. She, Stan, and John stood on the sidewalk. She'd thought about inviting everybody, but she decided they could do that later. It was about eight o'clock at night and dark outside, with a gentle snow and for once no wind. The streetlights were muted. Christmas lights were visible on some neighboring houses.

Their breaths puffing like miniature clouds, they walked up the shoveled stepped sidewalk to a deep front porch and a solid oak door with leaded glass. Sconces on either side of the door lit the entrance— original brass, it looked like, tarnished but solid.

"I probably should have skimped on the materials. It would've helped the margins. But I'm a sucker for a good house."

Stan looked at her and shook his head slightly. "Open the door."

Claire fumbled with the key and let them inside. The entry was formal, hexagonal ceramic tiles with a closet to each side, with french doors into the living room. Heavy Craftsman-style oak, stained dark, framed the room, which had a built-in leaded glass cupboard and a dark-green ceramic fireplace. "The fireplace works, but I have it shut off. Whoever buys it can decide if they want an insert."

Claire led him through the bedroom, bath, kitchen, and formal dining room. "It's forty by forty on this level, sixteen hundred square feet. I figure with two staircases, it'd be a cinch to set it up as three separate units—one upstairs, one here, and the other in the basement using the walkout as the entrance."

The rooms echoed. There was no furniture. Polished wood floors gleamed and squeaked quietly as they walked through the house. Stan was quiet, impressed, taking it all in.

They ended in the basement. Solid new foundation walls allowed for a more modern look, with a few historic features to tie in with the rest of the house. Heavy five-panel doors, brass knobs, and substantial millwork enhanced a complete kitchen, bath, two rooms, and a gas fireplace by the walkout entrance.

"It's not the best part of town right now, but I think it will be. There are three renovations on this block alone, close to downtown. I think you could rent out two of the three and break even on the payments. Maybe even rent the loft above the garage—might be nice for a single guy." She paused. "For whoever buys it."

Stan stopped and looked at her. "You like this house?"

Claire hitched the baby on her hip. He was a solid little guy. "I like the *idea* of this house."

Slowly, Stan turned around, looking at a place that seemed permanent and solid, wondering if a home and lifestyle like this was really possible. In the quiet of the room, they could hear the bells of the downtown cathedral, chiming out a carol.

Merry Christmas.

Chapter 78 - Deidre Hall

It was the morning of Christmas Eve, and Deidre Hall was exhilarated. Today was the day, or perhaps more accurate, tonight was the night. Like a chess master examining the remaining pieces on the board, she went over her plan. In one or two moves, it was checkmate. Life was not like chess, of course. People were more varied and their moves more complex. But the important pieces, Harrison and LaFave, were as predictable as gravity. That was the exhilarating part—to move and manipulate, to cause pain and suffering and have people helpless to stop it, all because of their stupid predictability. Stan Martin would die that night, not because he would fall to his death but because he would willingly, oh so willingly, climb his way hundreds of feet to do it.

She gave a brilliant white-toothed smile and kissed LaFave, the instrument of her torture. "Come on, lover. Let's go get the baby."

Chapter 79 - Claire

Traffic was at a greasy standstill. At five o'clock Christmas Eve, snow like wet goose feathers was falling, beautiful to behold and a mess to drive through. There were four inches on the ground—nothing for most Sioux Falls drivers, who were used to five months of lousy driving conditions, but Tenth Street was a steep hill with a stoplight in the middle of it. Traffic was forced to stop then had to claw its way uphill, tires polishing the snow to packed ice. Cars with old tires or bad traction would lose faith and snarl the trip for everyone.

Bang. She felt the impact before she registered the cause. *A shopping cart?* Lewis Drug was to her right, and it looked like some jerk had taken a shopping cart from the lot and pushed it between stalled cars, eventually hitting hers. She sighed in frustration. If she left it there, it would only cause more trouble for others. She'd better get it out of the way, while traffic was stopped.

"Hang on, little man," she said to John, who sat in his car seat, looking as frightened as she'd ever seen him. "Don't worry, buddy, it's only snow. Mommy'll be back in a jiff."

Claire unhooked her seatbelt, got out of the truck, and corralled the cart, which was dented and covered in slush. Motioning to the cars behind, she pushed the cart quickly off to the side, jumped it up the curb and onto the sidewalk, then tipped it over like a calf at a roping contest in case it tried rolling into traffic again.

Then she dodged back, slipped behind the wheel, buckled up, and released the parking brake just as traffic started moving. "Here we go, John! We'll go pick up Daddy and head on home!" She looked in her rearview mirror to reassure him.

The car seat was empty.

Chapter 80 - Stan

It was five thirty on Christmas Eve, and Stan was cleaning up and getting ready to leave. There was not much for news. Jim Fletcher was working on a piece about farmers buying equipment before year-end as a tax write-off, which would be more interesting to Sioux Falls listeners once Jim could quantify the economic impact in dollars and cents. And Gretchen Wallace was working on a holiday shopping poll of which stores offered best customer service, interesting for this time of year. Maybe it could become an annual story.

Stan glanced at the clock. He and Claire had decided to go to the candlelight service that evening at the nearby church, a conversation that apparently both had put some serious thought into.

"We should go to church tomorrow," Claire had said at bedtime as she and Stan were at the edge of sleep.

Stan had his own thoughts but wanted to know hers. "Why?"

She sighed. Stan thought she'd drifted off, but after a few moments, she murmured, "Because of my dad. Because of John. Because of you… because if we don't go, then what's the point?"

Stan had nodded against her back, spooning her. "I agree."

So they were going to church, and Stan felt a ridiculous urge to sing—something he was very bad at—when the phone rang to his desk.

"Stan Martin, KCAH."

The voice at the other end was strained and broken, hard to hear because of the static. "Y-You… fucker." Stan had been sworn at before and was ready to hang up when the voice continued. "Before I kill myself and your kid, I thought I'd introduce myself as the man you ruined."

Stan's heart chilled and stopped. *Did he say "your kid"?*

"I am Harrison Benjamin Hall the Fifth, MD. At least for a little while longer. I thought I'd make this a most memorable holiday by jumping and taking your dear little boy with me."

"You have my son?" Stan said in a choked voice.

He heard staticky laughter.

"Where are you?" Stan asked.

"Four hundred feet…" The man's voice was trembling.

"Wait! Hang on! No need to do this… just tell me where you are, and we can get through this."

The laughter came back, high and unhinged. "Weather ball red, soon we'll both be dead." There was more static…

Stan threw down the phone and ran from the building.

Chapter 81 - Doris

Doris was at the radio station, working on some year-end stuff, ready to call it quits for the holiday and feeling troubled about Stan's behavior.

Claire came racing into the building. "Where's Stan?"

"He left. What's wrong? He seemed terribly upset."

"It's John! Someone stole him out of the back seat of the truck on Tenth Street. Call the police and let them know. Where is Stan?"

Doris's heart stopped. "John? Little John? Oh my God."

"Where is Stan?" Claire asked again. "Where did he go?"

Doris's thoughts were tumbling over each other as she tried to grasp what was being said. "He, uh, he ran out of here a few minutes ago. He said something about the weather ball."

"The weather ball?"

"Uh, yes. They used to tell the weather with it."

"What about it?" Claire looked frantic.

"Uh, well, he said, uh, he needed to drive out to the tower and see someone, something about stopping a crime…" Suddenly, tears welled up in her eyes. "Oh my gosh, do you think this has something to do with John?"

Claire blanched. "Call the police." And then she ran out the door into the snow.

Chapter 82 - Stan

The snow was falling in deep clots as Stan raced to the transmitter site. Not an ideal winter car, the Shark slipped and swerved from side to side, almost throwing Stan into the ditch. Up ahead, the beacons on the tower flashed red… off… red… off. He made a left turn, and the Shark followed the ruts in the snow, struggling to gain ground, finally slowing to a stop in the slog of snow.

He pushed the door open into a drift and climbed out, frantic. The he leapt through the drifts down the drive toward the transmitter shack. Near the door was an unknown car, an SUV, proof of something he dreaded.

He heard a sobbing scream as he got near the open door. "Noo! Please, Gawd, save him!"

Bursting in, he saw the wretched woman, red-faced and tearstained.

"Oh please, save him! He's insane!" The blond woman clutched at him, pulling on his sleeve hysterically.

"Who?"

"It's my stepson, my beloved Benjy! You've ruined him! Ruined him… and he… he's going to jump!"

"Jump. Jump where?"

"I tried to stop him… it's all your fault… you and your stupid radio story. You did this!"

"Did he have a young child, a baby, with him?"

The woman melted into the floor, sobbing, fists pressed into her eyes.

Stan lifted her up and shook her, shouting, "Did he have a baby with him?"

Swollen, teary green eyes looked up at him. She grabbed him for support.

"Oh, save him, please! Save my Benjy!"

Frantic, Stan grabbed a climbing harness and headed for the door.

Chapter 83 - Deidre Hall

Lifting herself from the floor of the radio shack, Deidre Hall rearranged her hair and adjusted her clothes. She listened for a second then walked outside to check the tower. Snow was falling in clumps. She could see the red lights glowing on the tower. Shielding her eyes from the falling snow, she peered up, looking for...

There he is! Yes, it was Stan—she was sure of it. Surprised, she could see that he was already about fifty feet up the tower and still climbing. She ran back inside and located the jack switch, gray and substantial. The handle was pointing to the white Off sticker, safety protocol for anyone on the tower. Reaching up, she grabbed the handle and threw the switch to On. *A little insurance.*

She wheeled around and headed to the SUV to get the bolt cutters to finish the job completely.

Chapter 84 -Stan

The wind. Always the wind. Calm during much of the day, it had now picked up to about thirty miles an hour, moaning through the guy wires as Stan climbed up, up, up. Heart pounding, thighs burning, he grabbed and slipped then grabbed again. He looked down and almost panicked. The ground was gone in the darkness, swirls of snowflakes whirling by into nothingness. Climbing a tower rung upon rung was more than dangerous—it was also hard physical work and, for one not used to it, a quick way for an unsteady foot to slip. Pausing, Stan forced himself to breathe and slow down a bit. *Pace yourself.*

The rubber gloves were cold and unwieldy. The climbing harness cut into his crotch, restricted his shoulder movement, and impeded the motion of his legs, but adjusting the straps was far from his mind. *Don't look down.*

The tower consisted of three upright steel rods about two feet apart from each other, and connecting the uprights was a series of welded triangles. Theoretically, it was the most rigid of structures, but as he climbed, he could feel it sway in the wind. He reached a juncture in the tower where impossibly thin guy wires were attached, stretching down and away into the darkness, and the color of the tower changed from red to white. Unwillingly, Stan remembered that meant he'd climbed another seventy feet. His legs trembled violently from the exertion, and his breath came in ragged puffs, his heart in his throat, as he peered up into the tower heights, chasing after his son.

Nearing the top, Stan could feel the tower sway in the wind two or three inches. *Shit.*

There! In the glow of the blinking lights, Stan could make out the base of the platform at the top of the tower and the small booth that the crazed Dr. Hall was in.

He called up to the tower from below the base. "Dr. Hall! It's okay! I'm Stan Martin. I just want to talk to…"

Suddenly, a length of chain came slapping down and crashed an inch away from Stan's right hand. *Clang!* Stan's foot slipped, and for a sickening second, he hung from two rubber gloves off of the half-inch-thick steel supports.

A head appeared three feet above him, grimacing down at him. The red light of the tower beacon pulsed, and for a second, Stan could see him. The form, the posture… something told Stan it was the man from Claire's video, the man in the Hall Cable TV van.

Clang! The chain lashed down again, a painful glancing blow to his knuckles.

A trap! The fool is trying to kill me!

Stan stepped down the tower three steps and paused, hooking the carabiner of his safety harness to the tower support. The face looked down at him again. He was wearing a similar harness to Stan's and hooking his own carabiner to the chain—Stan could see him jump off the tower feetfirst, swinging wide, heading for him.

Stan dodged to the edge of his tether but was still struck. It was only a glancing blow, yet Stan lost his footing and fell one foot before the harness he was wearing jarred him to halt, his heart in his throat.

The wind moaned through the wires, the click of the tower lights switching on and off, so that the frenzied battle was fought in ten-second increments of complete darkness or garish red light.

Bigger and stronger, the stranger now had the back of Stan's harness in his grip and was looping behind him, clutching him around the waist with his legs, wrapping his arms around Stan's throat from behind.

Pulsing fear made Stan's own heartbeat the loudest sound and, after that, the harsh breath of the man behind him. Then he had a sense of being kicked sideways. The entire tower jolted, a sickening sudden shift of six inches, pulling Stan back into the man. Questions of why this had happened were answered in a millisecond with a *Tching!*—the metallic snap of a guy wire being broken.

Realization hit Stan in a cold rush. "The tower…!" Stan kicked furiously back with his heels. "It's going to fall!"

The tower beacon's red flash lit up the darkness. The man did not know or seem to care what Stan said. He dug his forearm under Stan's chin and pulled back, trying to rip Stan away from his grasp of the tower.

There was darkness as the beacon shut off, another shuddering kick, and *Tching*! The tower swerved with a drunken lurch, this time more immediate—Stan could feel the tower sing like a metal key struck by a mallet. The man behind him must have understood what was happening because he suddenly loosened his grasp, allowing Stan to twist and escape. Facing the man, he struck out blindly to where his face should be. The red light flashed on, and Stan could see in harsh red light the reason his adversary had stopped struggling. An astonished pair of eyes stared blankly at him underneath a forehead mostly gone, sliced cleanly away by the whiplash of the broken guy wire.

Stan gasped.

And then as had happened just once before in his life, Stan found himself transported into a place of complete clarity, his situations and options laid out before him in slow motion where they could be decided upon with dispassionate reason.

The tower was starting to topple. The wind pushing against him and the corpse in front of him were slowing its fall, but he could already feel the tilt. There was no way to climb down—he was certain to fall four hundred feet to his death, crushed into the frozen earth by a toppling tower.

Click. The red light turned on one last time. Acting quickly, Stan decoupled his carabiner from the tower and clipped it to the carabiner of the dead man's harness. Then he heaved up and decoupled the dead man from the tower. Both men started falling. Using a final kick, Stan pushed away from the tower, launching them both out and away as he and the dead man plunged into darkness.

Chapter 85 – Deidre

It was fascinating. As soon as that fool Stan Martin headed up the tower, Deidre Hall had trotted back the SUV and grabbed the bolt cutters out of the back seat. Stepping purposefully, she made it to the chain-link fence surrounding the guy-wire anchor. She looked up, and in the flash of the tower lights, she could see that Stan Martin was already about two-thirds of the way up the tower. *Better hurry.*

She turned back and clipped her way through the fence wire, *clip, clip*. It had taken about a full minute to cut her way through the fence, resisting the temptation to see how far Stan had climbed. *Plenty of time.*

Now she was through the fence and standing next to the guy wires. She could hear them hum and thrum in the wind. Surprisingly thin, the stranded wire was no match for the cutters. She picked the second one and cut it. *Tching!* She laughed. It sounded like a science-fiction gun. The wire whipped up and away like a rubber band. From a distance, she could see the tower stagger a bit, lurching like an enormous wounded insect. *Cool.*

Now for the fun part. Picking carefully, she cut the top wire. *Tching!* The wire whipped away into the darkness like a broken guitar string. The top third of the tower swayed drunkenly then slowly toppled away from her, down, down to the ground. She could not see either LaFave or Martin fall, but her breath quickened at the thought of the terror of their last moments. Hopefully, she could find them in the wreckage. She was curious to see what happened to them.

Chapter 86 - Claire

Claire saw the tower lights fall and crumple as she swerved into the tower driveway, shouting in anguish, "Noo!" She opened the door next to Stan's abandoned car, stumbled out of the pickup, and ran into the blowing snow, plunging through the drifts. "Stan!"

She was not the first on the scene. Out of nowhere, a sobbing woman with blond hair was pointing hysterically. "They're over there! Hurry!"

As Claire pivoted to look, the very back of her mind asked a question that took too long for her conscious to form. *Why was that woman here before me?*

There was a crushing, blinding blow to the back of Claire's head, and she fell unconscious into the snow.

Chapter 87 - Stan

The fall through darkness had only lasted three seconds—three heart-stopping pitch-black seconds that seemed like an eternity. Later, Stan looked it up in a physics book that told him that the acceleration of a three-second free fall meant he hit the guy wire at thirty miles an hour. In his memory, the fall was much, much longer, the speed much, much faster. He'd felt a sudden twanging jolt of shock and relief, the hope that when he pushed off and away from the tower, he'd aimed right, and the guy wire would land between him and the dead man.

Not quite. The body Stan was coupled to hit first at chest height, the guy wire catching it under the armpit, a garish scene lit up in vague red shadows. Then came a rip and a jolt. The first set of gray plastic blocks that prevented the electrical charge of the tower traveling to the ground caught the arm of the man, checking their speed, swinging Stan up and into the guy wire like a pendulum and striking a stinging blow to his cheek. With a rip, the two bodies were free. The force of the impact on the insulating block had ripped the dead man's arm loose, and the guy wires had caught the carabiners that still joined both of them. The wire sang as they started again in their dizzying descent, a macabre sort of downhill zip line.

Grabbing the lapels of the dead man, Stan pulled himself in tight and braced himself. Again, there was a jarring stop in midair when the carabiners ran into the last set of insulators.

The jolt and violent swinging slowed their descent but opened Stan to peril.

The tower was falling.

Or at least, the top two hundred feet were.

As the tower fell away from the broken guy wires, it descended toward Stan. The guy wires slackened, decreasing the slope of Stan's descent but keeping him within the range of the falling tower debris.

Drifts of fluffy wet snow started striking the feet and body of the corpse as the slackening guy wire raced to the ground. The chain-link fence that surrounded the anchors that held the guy wires was about eight feet tall and acted like a trampoline as Stan slammed sideways into it at thirty miles an hour. *Crack.* He felt a stab in his chest. *Broken ribs.* He knew the feeling well.

But the dead man and the snow and the chain-link cushion had saved his life. He lay there gasping. While he was catching his breath, the broken tower about fifty feet to his right started hissing menacingly in the snow, red lights still flashing.

Chapter 88 - Deidre

Stupid, she thought with grim satisfaction. She hefted the bolt cutters she'd used to hit the woman.

A blow to the head would be easier to explain if there was a bloody tower piece nearby. She walked to the transmitter shack, which was miraculously undamaged by the falling tower pieces. *There.* A segment about four feet long, jagged at the end, was sticking out of the snow. *Perfect.* She bent to reach it and remembered the danger of the tower. Stepping carefully, she entered into the shack and switched the switch to Off. *Much better.* Back outside, she reached down for the piece, bracing her hand against a crumpled segment of the tower.

An instant glaring heat burst out of her right wrist below where her hand had touched. It was a full second before she registered the shock. Suddenly, she realized what had happened—she'd been burned.

She jerked away then whirled and slipped, staggering against the same tower segment. Both ankles exploded with heat, her back and hips tingling like a funny bone only more painful.

Something must have been wrong with the power switch. She'd worry about that later. She had to hurry home before the police arrived. She needed time to think and prepare.

Halfway to her SUV, Deidre Hall felt nauseous. She collapsed and started vomiting. Her bowels cramped then let loose, staining the snow as she writhed in pain.

Chapter 89 - Cal

Wes and Cal were turning off Highway 106 when they saw the tower fall. Flooring the truck, Cal swerved down the road, noting that Stan's car and Claire's truck were already there.

"Hey, look." Wes pointed. Sure enough, a familiar white SUV was there too.

"Better shut 'er down."

Wes nodded as Cal stopped at the driveway. He hopped out and killed all power to the site. Only the tower lights continued to blink.

Chapter 90 - Claire

"Claire? Claire, you all right?"

With a searing pain, Claire opened her eyes, looking up into Stan's concerned face. Panic flared up. "Where's John?"

"Right here." Wes was plodding through the snow, carrying little John.

Whimpering slightly, the boy reaching down for Claire. Sitting up and stifling a cry of joy, Claire held him close. She sobbed with relief. John squirmed in her arms until he was facing her. He looked solemnly into her eyes, touching her cheek. Her pain seemed to go away.

"Where was he?" she asked.

Wes nodded. "Over in that sick gal's SUV."

Claire remembered the woman and the danger she'd caused. "Be careful! She's the one that hit me."

Cal smiled grimly. "Don't worry about that. She ain't gonna hurt anybody no more."

Wes nodded. "Nope."

Chapter 91 - Stan

It turned out that Stan and Claire and John did not go to the Christmas Eve service after all. Running on adrenaline, despite the pain in his ribs, Stan called the entire station together to explain the situation. Christmas Eve into Christmas day, writing through the night, KCAH's Christmas morning email headlines were astonishing:

"KCAH Tower Cut down by Deidre Hall, Wife of Harrison Benjamin Hall IV."

"Unknown Assailant, Linked to Deidre Hall, Attacks KCAH News Director."

"Unknown Assailant Decapitated by Cable of Collapsing KCAH Tower."

"KCAH News Director Survives Fall from Four-Hundred-Foot Tower."

"Deidre Hall Implicated in Kidnapping of KCAH News Director's Child."

"Deidre Hall Hospitalized with Severe RF Burns."

Every reporter got a by-line. The email letter caused a firestorm of reverberations through the city and even across the country. Fluff pieces about after-Christmas shopping and Salvation Army donations were swept aside as the unbelievable stories of murder, cover-up, and corruption spread across the country.

But as astounding as all of that news was, a different story, shocking in its own way, was released just six hours later: "KCAH Disbanded. Employer Fires all Employees, Building Shuttered."

Chapter 92 – Cal

It was still Christmas Day, so you couldn't blame the police for leaving the tower unguarded. The trouble was over, and the police tape was in place. Cal and Wes stepped carefully around the tape and walked purposefully toward the transmitter shack. If asked, they would claim innocence, just a couple of radio techs following up after a tower collapse. The chain-link fence around one of the guy-wire anchors was cut, and inside the fence, two of the guy wires, cut clean through, could be seen.

Wes nodded. *Thought so.*

Continuing to the shack, Cal opened the door and looked around. The coast was clear. Nodding to Wes, Cal stepped inside toward the jack switch.

Days before, they'd had a conversation about a beautiful blonde with green eyes who probably was harmless but might be very dangerous. Since Cal and Wes were the only ones who were supposed to have access to the shack, they'd decided a little experiment might be in order to see if their suspicions were confirmed.

Wes carefully peeled loose the On and Off labels of the jack switch and placed them back where they belonged. Back in the truck, Cal broke the silence. "That was one evil woman."

Wes nodded. "Yep."

Chapter 93 - Harrison Hall

The Sioux Falls Regional Airport was small by most standards, no noise or hubbub, just people going about their business, traveling to Vegas and Orlando for fun and Chicago and Minneapolis for business. The day after Christmas, travel would be busy, but Harrison Hall wasn't worried. The charter was a direct flight that would take him over the mess of O'Hare or other points between.

The plane had been deiced, and he was waiting for takeoff when he noticed the flashing lights. *Interesting.* Craning his head, he was able to see the police cars heading down the runway and around from behind the terminal. He looked for the smoke of a fire. Maybe another plane was in trouble. The cars came closer and stopped by the plane. Policemen jumped out and ran. Maybe it was a hostage situation. He hoped he was safe.

Moments later, the sealed door of the plane was opened, and a detective in plain clothes walked carefully toward him. "Dr. Hall? You are under arrest for suspicion of murder." After reciting something about Hall's rights, he put cuffs on his wrists and escorted Hall off the plane.

Chapter 94 - Stan

It was New Year's Eve. All the former KCAH staff was gathered at Stan and Claire's house. Pizza boxes, cases of beer, and cans of soda were scattered about the floor. A fire roared in the fireplace.

Matt Bradley's uncle owned a furniture store and had let Matt haul in some chairs and couches and a few coffee tables and a stereo. The mood was bittersweet, as everyone knew what was about to happen and that, as the saying went, all good things must come to an end.

Stories were swapped, details and perspectives shared. They discussed the truly evil nature of the woman known as Deidre Hall. Her diagnosis was grim as her health continued to deteriorate. She was puffed and bloated and in extreme pain. Death from radio-frequency electrocution was days away.

"That is the thing that doesn't make sense." Stan was shaking his head. "Why did she deliberately touch a hot tower?"

Wes and Cal looked at each other. Cal shook his head slightly.

Don Keshane piped up. "Here's what I wanna know… what the hell is Charlie Hofer getting away with? That asshole just gets to dump us on Christmas Day? What are we gonna do about it?"

Stan shrugged. "I can't say I'm surprised. When you get into business with a snake, you can expect to get bit."

Doris was sitting in a couch next to John Returns From Hunt. She had a wrapped cardboard box heavy enough that she had to slide it across the floor. "This is for you, Donnie. And maybe Matt. Stan, I suppose you may have some obligations based on the contract you signed with Charlie."

Curious, Donnie bent over the box. "Shit, it's heavy! What is it?" Not waiting for an answer, he opened the box to find it full of what looked like balance sheets, profit-and-loss statements, and more.

"This is… books? for Goodies?"

Doris shrugged. "Charlie is a creature of habit. I decided he might be up to something, so I've been doing a little dumpster diving. I bet you'll find something."

Matt was going over the papers. He whistled slowly.

Doris flashed a brilliant, victorious smile. "Merry Christmas, Charlie."

Chapter 95 - Everett Meyer

Everett Meyer was seated across from the federal prosecutor, trying to not feel uncomfortable.

"Mr. Everett, I'm Jim Hanson. We talked on the phone."

"Yes, and you are aware that I am here of my own volition to answer and help in your investigation of the Hall-Hauptmann Hospital. While I knew nothing of the events surrounding the tragic deaths and cover-up, I will try to help you in any way I can."

The speech was well rehearsed, and Hanson waited politely for him to finish. "That's great, swell. We really appreciate it. I suppose you've had a chance to think about what kind of legal malfeasance you might be accused of."

"Am I being charged with something? If so, this meeting is over, and I will seek counsel."

Hanson raised his hands. "No, no. No need for that. I'm sure you know the law as well as anybody. But there seems to be a possibility that the Halls got some sort of legal advice to help them circumvent the law, which could be construed as someone being an accomplice in a cover-up, and I'm asking—just asking, mind you—if you might be able to point in a direction of who might be bending the law beyond where it should go."

Meyer sucked in his breath and paused, considering his move. "Well, there is a junior associate with the hospital, Jessica Wright—a nice kid, really, but maybe a trifle… overzealous. I feel like she may have offered council to Benjamin Hall and Deidre Hall."

"Both deceased?"

Meyer shrugged. *Dead men tell no tales.*

"Maybe leading them in what to say?"

Meyer shrugged again. "She is very bright, perhaps lacking a certain moral compass."

Hanson sighed. "Any proof?"

Meyer spread his arms. "Hard to imagine leaving evidence so damning."

Hanson gave a disarming smile. "Yet you know it happens sometimes."

The door opened, and Jessica Wright entered along with a vaguely familiar man. Meyer felt a sudden sick feeling.

Hanson leaned forward. "So this is Jessica Wright. You know her, and you have probably met Spencer Thomas. He's the IT guy at Hall-Hauptmann, the one who sets up equipment, video recording"—Hanson put a tape on the desk—"audio recording…"

Meyer's sick feeling got worse.

Hanson shifted again in his seat. "You know, Mr. Everett, on second thought, maybe you'd better get that counsel."

Chapter 96 - Dr. Schneider

The room was dark, and the machines in the intensive care room beeped and whirred, keeping the patient alive hopefully long enough for more tests to be run. As a pathologist, Dr. Schneider was technically concerned with the processes of diseases and their cures, but there was no cure for radio-frequency burns, only a rare chance to document as much about the symptoms as possible, in the hopes of maybe helping diagnose future patients.

As he stepped closer, the smell of decomposition was unmistakable. Her wrists and ankles were bloated and grayish brown, with seeping wounds that followed the nerves up the forearms and calves. The theory might be that the nerve cells were more conductive to RF and, therefore, were the path the burns took. Dr. Schneider smoothed a hank of hair away from his pale forehead and suppressed his excitement.

The breath of the patient was rattling. She would need to be intubated soon to avoid suffocation. Since admittance, the patient had swollen to an alarming degree until her face and torso were bloated and blotched. Schneider guessed that up to twenty percent of her internal organs were cooked. *But which organs and how much?* Yes, he could find out many of these details in a postmortem, but there was so much more to learn while she was still alive.

Dr. Schneider looked carefully to make sure he was alone. Then he stepped close to the patient and pressed the flesh at her wrist. It dented in like gray bread dough, and the patient whimpered. *Cool.* Dr. Schneider leaned over the patient and whispered, "I wish you could tell me how much it hurt."

He pressed again. This time, he could see tears weeping out of her left eye, which was startlingly green next to the deep and mottled gray flesh. *Cool.*

Chapter 97 - Matt Bradley

Matt Bradley was in his aunt Judy's office. Still the same cluttered space, it hadn't changed a bit from when he was young enough to swing his legs from the edge of the battered leather armchair. He was collapsed into that chair, paper sack in hand, waiting.

"Quite a box of stuff there, boy-o." She studied him, looking down the rims of her glasses. "You hang around at strip clubs?"

"No, Aunt Judy, no. This is just a lead from a friend who knew I was an investigative reporter."

Aunt Judy let the glasses fall to the end of their chain, sniffed, and then put them back on the edge of her nose. She sniffed again.

"C'mon, Aunt Judy. You think I'd bring this stuff to you otherwise? You'd squeal to Mom in a second."

"Don't think I still won't, boy-o." She pulled a file from the top, a summary of what she'd found. She opened her mouth to speak and then shut it. Finally, she said, "You don't look so good, Matt. You look a little lunchy. No girl wants a lunchy-looking guy. If you want, I could take you down to Normans. They've got a sale on large and tall sizes. You'd look so good in a new blazer. Maybe some loafers—that way, you don't have to tie them." She looked pointedly at his untied tennis shoes.

Matt set his jaw and sighed.

His aunt raised her arms in surrender. "Okay, okay, the report."

A forensic accountant for the Justice Department, Judy Bauer was often called upon to testify at trial. As such, she was greatly feared—one, she could make technical stuff easy to understand, two, she was a natural teacher and a bit of a ham, and three, she was impossible to intimidate.

Staring at an invisible jury, she pushed her glasses up a notch and started preaching. "The first thing and the last thing is that embezzlers always get caught. If you write nothing down, cash only, you will get caught for not paying taxes. Ask Al Capone. If you write anything fake down, you still get caught—by me. Forensic accounting is the art and science of investigating people and money. Most people who run a set of false books write down numbers at random, skim a little off the top, and fudge the numbers enough to make it look good. And all I have to do is run a sample of numbers through Benford's Law and see what I can find."

Mat fed her the question, just like a friendly prosecutor. "What is Benford's Law?"

"Any group of numbers, no matter the size or origin, will start with the number one more than thirty percent of the time. And this paradox persists. Numbers start with one more often than two, and numbers start with two more than three, and so on. Numbers that start with nine are the least common of all."

"Any exceptions?"

"Well, when you're comparing just two numbers, the odds can fool you. But for this?" She patted the cardboard box full of spreadsheets, invoices, pay stubs, and tax documents and smiled grimly. "Not a chance."

"And?"

"Boy-o?" She pulled a graph off the top. "The normal Benford's Law graph is a nice curving slide from one to nine. Your pal Charlie Hofer has a graph that is all over the place. These numbers are funnier than Jack Benny, and it would definitely be worth a call to a buddy of mine at the IRS."

"Hang on a sec, Aunt Judy." Matt pulled a portable tape recorder out of the paper sack at his feet.

"You carry a recorder in a paper sack?"

Matt shrugged. "Can I get a few quotes before you call?"

Epilogue – Claire

It was spring, and Stan and Claire were walking along the sidewalk, a midmorning ritual they both enjoyed. The air was impossibly clean and fresh. Stan's ribs had healed, and John was able to walk, a sturdy little guy with a toddling gait. He was silent as ever, but Stan and Claire no longer worried about that.

"Meetcha at the café?" Stan nodded down the street.

"Sounds good." Claire walked John carefully across the street while Stan stopped by the post office.

A few minutes later, he slipped in across the table and sat down, looking at the menu. The nasty cut on his right cheek caused by sliding down the radio guy wire had healed to a muted purple, giving him a roguish look. *Right out of Central Casting.*

Claire saw the mail. "Anything good?"

"Got a letter from Doris."

"Yeah? Well, let's see it."

Stan handed the letter over, and Claire opened it:

Hey, Stan and Claire:

Hope you're doing well. We miss you both and Little John especially. Claire, you'll be happy to know that the place is rented, including the loft over the garage. We haven't had a lick of trouble since no one wants to mess with John even though he is a big softy. We've decided to keep renting the main floor and see what happens. You probably heard that Charlie has been indicted, and I should be glad, but I am mostly sad for him.

We wish you every happiness and think of you every day. Come and visit us soon!

Sincerely,

Doris Returns From Hunt

Stan studied Claire's face. "You okay?"

"Yeah."

"You think we made the right decision?"

Claire looked around at the people in the café. Right or wrong, good and bad, they were the people she was closest to. "Sure do."

Stan watched her with the same intense look he'd given her the first time she saw him walk into this same café in the small prairie town of Dansing, South Dakota. The same small thrill climbed her spine, followed by an urge to tuck a wisp of a curl behind her ear. "Whatcha want to order?"

Stan smiled. "I think I will have the biscuits and gravy."

Epilogue 2

At sentencing, Harrison Benjamin Hall IV's council had pleaded with the judge on point after point, losing every one. Finally, the last was a pitiful request that he not be incarcerated with the man who had implicated him, Everett Meyer.

The judge's smile was thin and malicious. He looked at Hall's council, shook his head, and then turned to look at Hall himself. "Sorry, Harrison."

The gavel fell, and so did Hall, taking the long, long road down from prestige and privilege into an orange jumpsuit and onto a drab green school bus. Once shackled in the bus, he and Meyer were driven up, up, up to the Federal Correctional Institution at Sandstone, a drab, depressing place, and he got his first look at the next ten to twelve years he would spend in northern Minnesota. The food there was horrible, the weather awful, and the cinder block cells were loud with the echoes of slamming doors, profane guards, and the relentless buzz of alarms. Alarms that told you when to get up. Alarms that told you to stand outside your cell for inspection. Alarms that told you when you could shower, when you could eat, and when you could shit. But the absolute worst punishment was psychological, and that was not carried out by the institution but by the prisoners themselves.

Hall was led into his cell, given his thin towel and blanket, and introduced to his cellmate. The beady eyes were instantly recognizable. They glittered with malignance.

Charlie Hofer spread out his arms in mock hospitality. "Welcome to the Country Club, Hallsey."

About the Author

Fast paced plots, unforgettable characters. The post-modern crime novels of JJ Gould feature gritty, real and often humorous characters caught in gripping and unpredictable situations. readers of JJ Gould find that heroes come from all walks of life and evil can live right down the street.

JJ Gould is a professional storyteller, speaker, broadcaster, podcaster, teacher and author. He can be reached through his website, ILikeThatStory.net